"We have to think of the children."

Ethan's eyes narrowed. "I am."

"I know you mean that, but—"

"There's nothing that'll prevent me from taking care of my brother's kids." He stood up. "And now I'm turning in. Good night."

After he left, Hannah sat there, thinking over every minute since he'd arrived in town.

Years ago Ethan had been a handsome daredevil who could make a girl fall in love and want to take off on wild adventures with him.

But he was different now. A man seasoned by the military. A man with a good heart who could be kind and gentle with kids and animals, yet who still possessed that charisma that drew her as much now as it once had.

But he was *not* the one who should have custody of the children.

No matter how strong it was, she had to put aside her attraction and focus on getting her sister's kids settled before the caseworker arrived.

And she had just thirty days to do it.

With Ethan watching every move.

A *USA TODAY* bestselling and award-winning author of over thirty-five novels, **Roxanne Rustand** lives in the country with her husband and a menagerie of pets, including three horses, rescue dogs and cats. She has a master's in nutrition and is a clinical dietitian. *RT Book Reviews* nominated her for a Career Achievement Award, two of her books won their annual Reviewers' Choice Award and two others were nominees.

Books by Roxanne Rustand

Love Inspired

Aspen Creek Crossroads

Winter Reunion
Second Chance Dad
The Single Dad's Redemption
An Aspen Creek Christmas

Rocky Mountain Heirs

The Loner's Thanksgiving Wish

Love Inspired Suspense

Big Sky Secrets

Fatal Burn
End Game
Murder at Granite Falls
Duty to Protect

Visit the Author Profile page at Harlequin.com for more titles.

An Aspen Creek Christmas

Roxanne Rustand

HARLEQUIN® LOVE INSPIRED®

LOVE INSPIRED BOOKS

Recycling programs for this product may not exist in your area.

ISBN-13: 978-0-373-71996-9

An Aspen Creek Christmas

Copyright © 2016 by Roxanne Rustand

www.Harlequin.com

Printed in U.S.A.

And we know that in all things God works for
the good of those who love Him,
who have been called according to His purpose.
—*Romans* 8:28

To Danielle, Ben, Lilly, Violet and Finn,
with all my love.

Acknowledgments

Many thanks to Dr. Erin L. Garman, DVM,
for her wonderful assistance with the veterinary
details in this story. Any errors are mine alone!

And also, many thanks to Lisa Mondello for her
research assistance on foster care and adoption.

Chapter One

Hannah Dorchester studied her travel-weary, disheveled niece and nephew sitting across from her in the McDonald's booth.

Neither had spoken since she'd picked them up at the Minneapolis–St. Paul airport a half hour ago, except to refuse every restaurant she could think of that might be open on Thanksgiving evening—hence, the fast food.

Though even in this child-friendly atmosphere they hadn't touched a bite of their meals. And no wonder. Today they'd faced yet another huge change in their young lives.

After they were orphaned seven months ago in Texas when their parents died in a head-on collision with a semi, their elderly great-aunt Cynthia in Dallas had been adamant about gaining custody.

But two weeks ago she'd tripped over a toy truck and broke her hip badly. She'd then informed Hannah she simply couldn't handle the children any longer—not while facing a long and painful recuperation.

Hannah had immediately begun the process of gaining out-of-state custody of the children. With a family law attorney at her side, she'd then gone to court to gain temporary guardianship.

Given that there were no other options besides Hannah or long-term foster care, social services and the court—bless them all—had expedited the process.

Scowling, Molly poked at the paper wrapping of her cheeseburger, then shoved it aside. "I don't even know why we had to come way up here. I don't *like* Wisconsin."

"You've never been here, honey." Hannah chose her words carefully. "It takes a long time to recover from a broken hip, and now Aunt Cynthia realizes she can't keep you and your brother any longer, because she… um…just isn't young enough to raise two children. But I know you're going to make some great friends here. And if you start missing her, maybe we can all go down for a visit—"

"She didn't even like us," Molly scoffed. "She was *mean*."

Hannah blinked. Cynthia was an elegant, austere woman who had never been particularly friendly during the few times Hannah had seen her. But *mean*? "Maybe she just isn't used to being around kids."

"She kept saying our uncle Ethan would be coming to take us, and he'd make us behave or else. 'Cause he's some kind of soldier."

Ethan?

Hannah swallowed hard, willing away the painful memories of the man she hadn't seen for thirteen years. A man she never, ever, wanted to see again. "I'm sure she didn't really mean—"

"Why would he want us? We never even met him." Molly angled an accusing glare at Hannah, then dropped her gaze to her lap. Her voice dropped to a whisper. "And even you didn't want us till now."

"I did, honey. Believe me. But Texas prefers to keep children in their home state, if possible, so they'll face less disruption. The judge decided Cynthia could provide a good home and keep you in your same schools."

Left unsaid was the fact that Cynthia, a wealthy widow who owned a major western wear company, kept a team of lawyers on retainer who had made very sure that her wishes were met. Hannah hadn't stood a chance in family court back then.

But now Cynthia's determination made more sense. Ethan was Cynthia's nephew. She'd apparently wanted to keep the children in Dallas, so the transition to his guardianship would be easier.

He'd probably even insisted on it.

Yet, seven months after the car wreck, he'd never showed up—no surprise there—and Cynthia was no longer capable, so now Hannah finally had a chance to give these kids the stable, loving home they deserved.

"We've got an hour drive ahead of us. Would you like to bring your food along?" she asked gently, wishing she could reach through the wall of grief surrounding them both.

Cole, only six years old, lifted his teary gaze briefly, shook his head and then slumped lower in his seat. "My m-mommy always h-had turkey an' everything on Thanksgiving."

His voice was so soft, so broken, that Hannah's heart clenched. "I know, sweetheart. But since you traveled today, I thought maybe we could have our big dinner tomorrow. Is that all right?"

The bleak expression in his eyes reaffirmed what she already knew.

This wasn't about the pumpkin pie or the holiday feast. It was about memories of happier times…and about loss. He just wanted his parents back.

And that could never be.

The next morning Hannah awoke early and made herself a cup of coffee, eager for the kids to wake up.

How life had changed in the blink of an eye—and how grateful she was for this wonderful blessing—a chance to finally surround her sister's children with love and healing.

Until two weeks ago she'd devoted herself to her career as a physician's assistant at the Aspen Creek Clinic and the ongoing renovation of this pretty little cottage on a hill north of Aspen Creek. Her only roomies had been the assorted rescue animals she took in, rehabbed and re-homed.

She'd had so much to arrange in a hurry after Cynthia's injury—both here and down in Texas—that there'd been no time to create a welcoming home for Molly and Cole. So they'd stayed a couple extra nights with one of Cynthia's friends while Hannah flew home to get the house ready.

Exhausted after their day of air travel and the sixty-mile drive from the airport, both children had been dazed and silent when she'd driven into her driveway at ten o'clock last night. They'd barely looked at their rooms before tumbling into bed without a whimper.

She'd checked on them several times during the night, but sometime during the early morning hours Cole had quietly dragged his quilt into Molly's room and went back to sleep wrapped up like a mummy on the floor at the side of her bed.

Hannah's stomach tightened. The poor little guy. Had he been scared? How had she failed to hear him?

Please, Lord, let this be an easy transition for them. They've been through so, so much.

A white-faced golden retriever limped to her side and bumped her hand, eliciting an ear rub. "So what do you think?" she whispered. "Will they be happy here?"

The dog, one of her rescues who had yet to find the perfect forever home, waved her flag of a tail and stared up at Hannah with pure adoration in her cloudy eyes. "I'd like to think you're telling me yes, Maisie."

The old dog crept silently into Molly's room and sniffed at Cole's makeshift sleeping bag, then gently curled up next to him.

The little boy stirred, mumbling something in his sleep. Cuddling closer to her warmth, he flung an arm over her soft neck.

Hannah felt her eyes burn at the dog's instinctive compassion. She'd started to tiptoe away when the puffy pink-and-purple comforter stirred on the bed.

Molly sat up and frowned as she surveyed the bedroom, her long, curly brown hair framing her face.

"Good morning, sweetie," Hannah whispered, stepping just inside the door. "What do you think of your new room?"

The walls were now a pale rose, the woodwork a crisp white. The bookshelves and a bedroom set were ivory with gold trim. Keeley, who owned an antique shop in town, had brought lovely lace curtains as well as a stained-glass lamp in pink, green and blue for the bedside table.

It was a fairy tale of a room that Hannah would have loved for herself as a child, but Molly just shrugged.

"Are you hungry for breakfast?"

Molly shook her head and flopped back down on her pillow, pulling the quilt up to her nose.

"Remember when I came to see you in Texas last time and made chocolate chip pancakes? I can make them this morning, or I have that chocolate cereal that you like."

"No." Molly yanked at the quilt to cover her head and turned toward the wall, clearly ending any further conversation.

Hannah tiptoed down the short hall to the kitchen, where a trio of cats sat staring at the refrigerator door, apparently willing it to provide an extra meal.

She stepped over a basset hound snoring in the middle of the floor, nudged the cats aside to grab a gallon of milk and then made her homemade version of a café-au-lait in her favorite mug.

Settling down at the breakfast bar overlooking the living room, she contemplated the stack of twelve, extra-large, newly delivered FedEx boxes sitting just inside the front door.

Each had felt like it had to weigh over fifty pounds when she'd dragged them in from the porch. Each had given her a pang of sorrow.

They represented the remnants of her sister's life, after Cynthia had summarily sent all the adult clothing to Goodwill and hired an auction house to dispose of the apartment furnishings.

It was heartbreaking to think that everything left of the children's lives had been distilled into just twelve cartons.

The question now was how she should most tactfully deal with all of this without upsetting them. Would they cry at the finality of seeing those labels and the contents? Things they'd seen in their old home, before a drunken truck driver had plowed into their parents' car and everything went so terribly wrong?

Hannah pushed away from the breakfast counter and moved over to the boxes to read the labels written in Cynthia's elegant hand.

Hannah quickly stowed Dee and Rob's boxes out of sight in her own bedroom closet to consider later. Then she lugged one of the Home Office boxes across the living room and began searching for school and health records, categorizing the contents into neat piles on the sofa.

At a knock on the door she looked up, startled at the silhouette of a tall, broad-shouldered man standing outside the front door. The basset hound gave a single, bored woof and went back to sleep.

She was usually working at the clinic during the day, so none of her friends would think to visit her at this time of the morning. It was probably just another shipment of boxes from Cynthia—who must have paid a fortune for such quick delivery.

She pulled back the lace curtain to look outside before unlocking the dead bolt.

She froze. It was Ethan Williams.

And he'd *seen* her. There was no way she could step away from the door and pretend she wasn't home.

From all the way down in Texas—or wherever it was that he'd been—Ethan had somehow found her, deep in this pine forest, five miles out of Aspen Creek on a winding gravel road.

He was the last person she'd ever wanted to see again. The cruelest man she'd ever met. And she knew his arrival spelled just one thing.

Trouble.

* * *

One glance at Hannah's horrified expression through the multipaned window in the door and Ethan knew his chances of being allowed inside were slim to none.

He deserved that and worse. But he'd traveled a long way. This visit wasn't about the troubled history between them. It was about the kids and their welfare, and he knew he had to handle this carefully or there'd be a battle every step of the way. It wasn't one he planned to lose.

After a long moment of hesitation, Hannah closed her eyes briefly, as if saying a silent prayer, then cracked the door open without releasing the safety chain. She focused her gaze somewhere above his left shoulder. "Yes?"

He drew in a jagged breath.

She was even more beautiful than when he'd seen her last—thirteen years ago. Slim, shapely, with honey-gold hair that fell to her shoulders in waves and startling, light blue eyes.

They'd first met at his brother Rob's wedding rehearsal, and their mutual attraction had been immediate. He hadn't taken his eyes off her for a second during the rehearsal and wedding, and despite all the years since then, he now felt that same rush of emotion all over again.

From a lifelong habit he nearly offered his right hand—or what was left of it—but caught himself just in time. "It's been a long time, Hannah. But you haven't changed a bit."

"If that's a compliment, don't think it will get you anywhere, Ethan. I've grown up since you last saw me and I'm not the fool I was when we first met. Understand?"

He nodded, edging the toe of his boot forward and bracing his left hand high on the door frame in case she tried to shut the door in his face. "Totally. Two adults. All business. That's fair enough."

"I can't imagine what business we would have after all these years." She bit her lower lip then reluctantly unhooked the safety chain. "Come in, but try to be quiet. The kids are still sleeping." She waved him past two tall stacks of boxes and toward a sofa and upholstered chairs arranged in front of a fieldstone fireplace.

The sofa was covered with stacks of papers, apparently taken from a shipping carton sitting on an ottoman, so he eased into one of the chairs, setting his jaw against the familiar stab of pain in his right knee.

Open suitcases stood just inside the door with children's clothing cascading out onto the floor, while a heap of winter jackets lay tossed over a chair.

Three cats, positioned like sphinx guardians in front of the refrigerator, glared at him from across the room.

"Nice place you have here," he said as he surveyed the warm amber walls and abundance of multipaned windows looking out into the timber.

"It's a mess right now. We got back from the airport pretty late last night."

"Beautiful country."

"I've got ten fenced acres, with state forest surrounding the house on three sides." She perched stiffly on the arm of the upholstered chair opposite his, still avoiding his eyes. "This is a perfect place to raise the kids. There's lots of room to play."

He ignored her pointed tone. "After coming up your road, I'm glad I chose an SUV instead of a sedan at the airport. You must not get much traffic up here."

She didn't return his smile. "There are only a few

homes on Spruce Road. I'm at the end of the line, actually. Public access to the government preserve is south of here. But I'm sure you didn't come all this way to discuss real estate."

"No." He'd rehearsed his speech during the flight north. Weighed different approaches. Honed his logic, to best make his points clear and get this done as efficiently as possible.

If only he'd returned to Dallas a few weeks sooner, before Cynthia's injury, the children's transition into his care would have gone smoothly. But from the steely glint in Hannah's eyes, he already knew *that* wasn't going to happen.

His conversations with Cynthia and social services in Dallas had made it clear that the situation was now far more complicated.

Maybe the children hadn't had time to settle in and bond with her, but Hannah had been granted temporary custody and had already brought the children north. He couldn't legally swoop in and whisk them back to Texas now—even though it was the right thing to do.

Unless he could convince her that it would be best for everyone involved. And why wouldn't she be relieved? The Hannah he remembered had been flighty, irresponsible. Surely she would understand that if he took the kids, her life would be a lot easier.

She crossed her legs and folded her arms over her chest. "Well?"

"I'm here to see Molly and Cole."

"Because…?"

"They're my niece and nephew," he said easily, "just as they are yours."

"You've missed them a lot, I'm sure." Her eyes narrowed. "Since you've seen them so often."

The ever-present phantom pain in his right arm began to pulse in deep, stabbing waves in response to his rising tension. "I've been overseas in the military. As you probably know."

"But you never went home to see your family? Not even," she added in a measured tone, her gaze fixed on his, "when the kids were born? Or your own brother's funeral? At least, I didn't see you there."

"I wasn't."

He hadn't been able to arrange for leave in time to fly back from the Middle East for the christenings. And as for the double funeral this spring...

He flinched as a cascade of images slammed through his brain. Gunfire. Explosions. Screams and blood and wrenching pain. And, finally, blessed darkness. That first long, hard and drug-fogged month at Walter Reed had left him incapable of anything more than simply existing.

"The kids say they've never met you."

"I saw Molly when she was toddler, and I made it back when Cole was starting to walk, but they were probably too young to remember. I plan to make that up to them, though."

"By finally finding time to visit them way up here?" The veiled note of sarcasm in Hannah's voice was unmistakable.

"Actually, now that I'm stateside, I want to take them back to Texas, where they belong."

"No." Her eyes flashed fire and she shook her head decisively. "I don't think so."

She'd definitely changed.

When he'd spent those three weeks with Hannah years ago, she'd been a fun, lighthearted nineteen-year-old with a sense of adventure and daring that matched his own.

Impulsive and giddy, she'd dared him to go cliff diving at the reservoir and had matched him shot for shot at a gun range. She'd invited him on five-mile runs in the moonlight, after the oppressive heat of those Texas summer days had faded.

She'd also been impetuous and immature, he'd realized in retrospect, though at the time he'd been sure she was his soul mate—if there was such a thing. He hadn't wanted to miss a minute of her company during the brief time he'd been stateside.

But now, instead of a sparkling sense of fun in her eyes, he saw only keen intelligence, absolute determination and a heartfelt wish that he would simply disappear.

After what he'd done to her, he expected nothing more.

But that didn't mean he was going to give in. No matter how difficult it was going to be, he owed it to Rob to make sure his kids were raised right, and were raised where they belonged.

"You do know that your custody is just temporary."

"That doesn't mean it will end. I spent considerable time with the children's caseworker, my Texas lawyer and in court. Even in a situation like this, involving out-of-state custody, the children's welfare and happiness are still paramount. So we'll have home visits and interviews by a caseworker after thirty days to evaluate how the kids are doing. Then again at three and six months—at which time I will petition for permanent custody and ultimately adopt them, if Molly and Cole agree."

He ground his teeth. Perhaps the nineteen-year-old he'd dated had grown up—but she was *not* the right person to take on this responsibility. "Clearly, there are lots of uncertainties. Is it fair to get them settled clear up here, when they'll need to move again?"

"That won't be the case."

He cleared his throat. "We need to straighten out this situation, the sooner the better. I honestly think they'd be better off coming back to Texas with me. You'd be free of responsibility, and they could be back in a familiar school, with their friends. Close to relatives and—"

Her smile vanished. "Close to what other relatives? Cynthia? Who didn't want to deal with them? And their uncle Ethan? Who travels the world? Who else is there to give them consistent day-to-day time and attention? Your dad is in a residential facility. Your mom and grandfather are gone. Would you need to hire a nanny for the months you're away?"

"What can you offer them?"

"A stable home. A *loving* home in the country with lots of animals and a huge fenced yard. I have lots of close friends with children they can play with. A warm church family. This is a friendly small town, where people know each other well and watch out for each other. Good schools. And," she added, meeting his eyes squarely, "I work at the Aspen Creek Clinic, so they'll have the best of medical care. I can guarantee it."

"It seems you've given this some thought."

"Since the day of the accident—not just when you showed up at my door. The kids don't even know you, Ethan. I heard Cole asking who you were and wondering why you'd never visited—at least that he could remember. Anyway, I'm their godmother—which ought to tell you something about their parents' wishes."

He snorted at that. "And I'm their godfather, so I guess we're even."

Her mouth dropped open. "I don't believe it. No one ever mentioned a thing about that. You certainly weren't at the christenings."

"I was stationed out of the country and couldn't make it back in time. I guess I was never able to make it back for anything important," he admitted with a twinge of regret. "But that doesn't mean I can't make up for lost time. And I plan to, even if it means that we need to take this back to court."

Hannah flung a hand in the air to silence him and glanced over her shoulder.

A little boy in Batman pajamas suddenly appeared in the arched doorway that probably led to the bedrooms, his hand on a white-faced golden retriever. He blinked at the sunlight streaming in through the wall of windows facing the driveway and forest beyond.

Hannah immediately went to him, kneeled and gave him a hug. "Good morning, sweetie. Did you have a good night's sleep?"

He rubbed his eyes and gave Ethan a brief, blank look, then regarded her with an achingly solemn expression. "Do we have to go back on the plane now?"

"No, of course not." She rested a gentle hand on his cheek. "Do you remember what your great-aunt Cynthia said before you left Texas?"

"She said we had to come here." His lower lip trembled and his eyes welled with tears. "But Mommy and Daddy are there, and our toys, and everything. And I *gotta* go back."

Chapter Two

Her heart breaking at Cole's grief and confusion, Hannah briefly closed her eyes. *Lord, please help me say the right things and help him understand. He's so very young for all of this to happen.*

"Your mommy and daddy will love you forever and ever, and would want to be with you more than anything," she said softly. "But they're in heaven now, sweetheart. When you grow very old and go to heaven, you'll be with them again, I promise."

She rested her hands gently on his shoulders and nodded toward Ethan. "But you have relatives on earth who love you very much, like your uncle Ethan and me. We want to make sure you are safe, and happy. And that you'll get to do all the fun things boys like to do."

She bit her lower lip, wanting to tell him that she would be the one to keep him safe and happy forever. But with Ethan lurking in a chair across the room, she couldn't risk adding more hurt to the little boy's life.

Would she even stand a chance against Ethan and his aunt if they challenged her custody in court? Could she afford enough legal representation to stop them?

"Your toys are in those boxes by the front door, and

I see you made friends with Maisie," she continued with a smile. "Did I tell you that there are lots of other friends here for you to meet?"

He met her eyes then dropped his gaze to the floor.

"Bootsie, the basset hound, is sleeping over there on the kitchen floor and the kitties by the fridge are Eenie, Meanie—the most playful one—and Moe. And outside I have some really fun surprises to show you once you get dressed and have some breakfast." She tipped her head toward the suitcases. "Do you want to pick out some clothes for today or should I?"

He lifted a shoulder in a faint shrug, so she dug through his suitcase and found jeans and a bright red sweatshirt. "Can you get dressed all by yourself?"

At that, his lower lip stuck out. "I'm six. Anybody in first grade can do that."

She chuckled. "Of course they can. So here you go, buddy. You can change in your room, okay? And I'll go check on your sister. Maybe she's ready to wake up, too."

After he dressed and she'd settled him at the counter with a bowl of cereal and a glass of juice, Hannah knocked lightly on Molly's door and stepped just inside when she heard no answer.

The eleven-year-old was dressed—in her clothes from yesterday—and huddled in the corner by the bed, her arms wrapped around her knees.

Hannah dropped to the floor next to her. "Tough morning, with all of these changes," she said softly. "I'm so sorry."

"I want to go *home*." Molly bit her lower lip. "But I don't know where that is anymore."

"You must feel like a leaf blowing in the wind. From

Texas to Oklahoma for a year, then back to Texas last April. Right?"

"'Cause Dad kept losing his jobs," Molly said bitterly. "But he said things would be better if we went back to Texas. He *promised.*"

Glancing through the open bedroom door, Hannah saw Ethan shift in his chair and frown at Molly's words. Had he known that little detail about his shiftless brother? About all the promises, all of the failures?

Probably not. At Cole's christening, her sister Dee had mentioned that Ethan rarely came back to Texas when on leave, and Rob had been adept at covering his failures with bluster and bravado.

With so little contact with his family, Ethan somehow imagined he should be the one to raise these kids? If he was like his brother, it would mean just one more chapter marked with disappointment in Molly's and Cole's lives.

"If you ever miss being with your great-aunt Cynthia, you can call her anytime. Or even visit her when she feels better."

"I don't miss her. Just home." Molly swallowed hard. "But now everything there is gone and there's no way we can go back. It would never be the same." Molly glared at Hannah. "You won't ever be our mom. I'll *never* call you that."

"Of course not. When you were little, you called me Auntie Hannah." Hannah rested a comforting hand on Molly's, but the child jerked her hand away. "You can call me Aunt Hannah or just Hannah. Does that sound okay?"

Molly gave a faint, dismissive shrug.

"Sweetheart, I loved my sister very much, and I don't

want to take her place. I just want you to be happy again someday."

"Then I need to be with my old friends at school. Not here." Molly dropped her forehead to her upraised knees.

With all the times her family had moved in the past three years, Hannah knew the poor girl had barely had the time to make new friends before changing schools and starting over. Though she wasn't ready to hear it, Aspen Creek would be her first chance to actually put down roots.

"Speaking of friends, I have some for you to meet—right here."

Molly shuddered. "I'm not staying and I don't *want* to meet anyone."

Hannah rose. "I think you'll feel differently in a moment. After breakfast, we'll have some introductions. Okay?"

"I don't *like* breakfast."

Hannah had known there'd be plenty of problems ahead, and that choosing her battles would be the key to making this work. Today's breakfast just wasn't one of them.

Cole finished his cereal, then swiveled in circles on his bar stool several times before pulling to a stop and pinning his gaze on Ethan. "You're my uncle?"

Ethan nodded.

Cole's eyes narrowed. "I never met you."

"That's because I'm usually very far away." Ethan cleared his throat. Did he explain that he was Rob's brother or would mentioning the kid's dad make him cry?

He'd always been uneasy around children, never having a clue what to say. If he upset the boy, would it make everything even more difficult in the future?

He definitely didn't want to mess this up on the first day.

He summoned a smile. "You did meet me, Cole… but you were just a little guy then."

From Cole's stubborn expression, he wasn't buying it. "If you're my uncle, how come you didn't come see us all the time like Hannah? She came lots of times on a plane, and even brought us presents. Every time."

"Well, I couldn't come to see you often because I'm a soldier. So I've been gone a lot, way on the other side of the world."

"Shooting guns and stuff like on TV?" The boy's eyes widened with worry and a touch of fear. "Do you kill people for *real*?"

"Uh…" He searched for the right thing to say to the boy, who slid off his stool and backed up beside Hannah, and figured a vague answer was best. "Soldiers do a lot of things—not just fight."

Cole considered that for a moment, his expression still wary. "So I could take you to show-and-tell, with your guns and everything?"

Ethan shuddered at that. "That would not be a good idea, buddy. Guns aren't safe—especially at school."

He looked up and found Hannah glaring at him, her arms folded over her chest and her eyes as cold as steel.

"You can thank your aunt Cynthia for how he feels about you. Apparently she told Molly and Cole that you were a tough guy. One who would really straighten them out. If you ever showed up, anyway."

"Why on earth would she—" He heaved a sigh, suddenly knowing all too well.

Even when he and Rob were kids, she'd been a stickler about her designer clothes, her elegant lifestyle. She'd always watched them like a hawk during their rare visits to her pristine home. Having Rob's two kids underfoot all those months had probably been unbelievably stressful for a woman who had always prized perfection over warm family emotions.

Ethan cleared his throat, searching for a different topic. "So, do you, um, like to ride bikes?"

"Don't got one." The child's face fell, his eyes filled with stark grief. "Mom said she'd get me a bike after we moved. But she died."

"I—I'm…" The boy's words felt like a fist to Ethan's gut and he floundered to a halt. "I'm so sorry about that."

Knowing Rob, there probably hadn't been any extra money for a new bike anyway, even though Ethan had loaned him a lot of money over the years.

His brother had always had just one more emergency, one more bout of overdue bills, and promises that it wouldn't happen again. And, always, a case of amnesia when it came to paying any of it back.

"I'm not batting a thousand here, am I?" Ethan muttered, looking up at Hannah.

"Nope." Her eyes narrowed on him. "And just in case you haven't noticed, never think this situation is easy."

Cole looked between them, clearly confused by their exchange.

"Time for a new topic," Hannah muttered as she put Cole's bowl and cup in the sink. She smiled down at him. "We have our first snowstorm of the year predicted on Sunday, so right now I think we should be shopping for sleds. But come spring I'll make sure you and your sister have new bikes. Now—are you ready for a surprise?"

His eyes round and serious, Cole nodded.

Molly appeared in the kitchen, her expression dour, and Ethan felt his heart clench at seeing her long, curly brown hair and big green eyes. Cole was fair and blond like his mom, but Molly was nearly identical to her dad at that same age—even down to her stubborn chin, the sprinkle of freckles over her nose and slender frame.

"Stay where you are, so you don't get trampled. I'll be right back." Hannah went through a door leading into the attached garage, leaving it open behind her.

A moment later a river of puppies exploded into the kitchen. Black ones. White ones. Gold. Spotted and speckled. They tumbled across the floor with squeals of excitement and chased each other throughout the kitchen and living room. The basset snored on.

Giggling, Cole dropped to the floor, quickly overcome with puppies trying to crawl over his legs. But though a glimmer of a smile briefly touched her lips, Molly held on to her aloof expression and backed away.

Ethan winced as a white pup with a black spot over one eye careened against his bad right ankle then landed in a heap on his other foot.

Forgetting his usual caution, he reached down and scooped it up, cradling its fat bottom in his good hand to look into its pudgy face. "Who are you, little guy?"

"I haven't named any of them yet," Hannah said. "That might be a good job for Molly and Cole."

She glanced at Ethan's weak ankle, where his brace probably showed beneath the hem of his jeans, and cocked her head, obviously curious but too polite to ask. But when she lifted her gaze, her attention caught on his prosthetic hand and her mouth dropped open. She quickly looked away. "I…I didn't realize. I'm so sorry, Ethan. Are, um, you all right now?"

Unwanted attention.

Shallow sympathy.

Platitudes.

He gritted his teeth. After leaving the hospital he'd encountered those reactions at every turn and he wanted none of it.

He knew he was fortunate to still have both legs. Fortunate to finally be walking unaided and to have a state-of-the-art prosthesis that once again made him a functional human being.

But he still struggled with a surge of instant resentment whenever he saw pity in someone's eyes. So many soldiers had to deal with far worse and deserved sympathy far more than he did. And all too many—some of the best friends he'd ever had—never had a chance to come home.

He shrugged off her sentiment and surveyed the puppy pandemonium. "This is like trying to count minnows in a bucket. How many of them are there?"

"An even dozen." She hitched her chin toward the garage. "The mom was a stray and she was brought here just before she whelped."

"Quite a bonanza."

Hannah picked up two of the black-and-white-spotted pups and snuggled them against her neck. "Not a record litter, but more than enough. She'll be spayed before I try to find her a good home."

Molly looked up at Hannah. "They all live here?"

"Not in the house. The mom and pups have a fenced cage, heat lamp and warm bed in the garage, with a doggie door out to the fenced backyard. I bring the little guys inside for socialization several times a day and give their poor mom a break." Hannah grinned at her. "Now that you're here, you can help me play with them. I have more friends to show you, but that can wait until I do chores."

Now Molly had a half dozen of them crawling over her feet and when she crouched, they tried to lick her face. "You have even more puppies?"

"No…not right now. But there are some other rescues in the barn."

The joy of the romping puppies was too infectious not to elicit a smile and Ethan found himself chuckling at their antics. "Isn't there a humane shelter in town?"

"On the other side of the county, but not anywhere close to Aspen Creek. So there are several of us who try to help. We have fund-raisers every year to help with food, spaying, neutering and vaccinations."

Two of the pups started chasing each other around the living room, skidding on the hardwood floors and braided rugs. One of them scrambled onto the sofa and scattered the stacks of paper like falling leaves in a stiff wind.

Molly's smile faded as she focused on the big card-board box by the sofa. "'Rob and Dee's home office and health records,'" she read aloud. She turned to give Hannah an accusing look. "You're snooping through my mom and dad's stuff?"

Hannah paled at her harsh tone. "I wasn't snooping, honey. Cynthia collected all of their important papers and sent them to me. They came this morning. We'll need your health records and other documents for when we get you set up with a doctor, dentist and the school."

Molly's mouth hardened. "Well, if you think you're gonna find money or something, good luck with that, because we didn't have any. Sometimes Mom didn't have enough money for the grocery store. Not even at Christmas, and that made her cry."

Ethan tensed, remembering all the times his brother had asked him for loans. Had things been even worse for them than Rob could admit? "I'm so sorry. If I'd known…"

Hannah glanced up at him with a frown, then gave the children a faint smile. "You know what? I think these pups would love to run and play with you two in the backyard. Want to grab your jackets? Then after you're done playing, I want you to meet Penelope."

She had the kids bundled up and the whole lot of them—exuberant puppies and kids—outside in minutes. He'd watched every move and still didn't know quite how she'd done it with puppies running everywhere and Cole too excited to stand still.

Cole ran around the yard with the pups, though Molly perched on a picnic table and chewed her fingernails, doing her best to look bored.

Despite the awkward history between them and his determination to take the kids back to Texas, Ethan couldn't help feeling a newfound appreciation for Hannah as they stood on the back deck to watch the melee. "You're good with them."

"Never had any of my own, of course, but one learns." She shrugged. "Corralling kids when armed with vaccination syringes does take some practice."

"You mentioned the clinic earlier. Are you a nurse?"

"I'm a PA—physician's assistant."

He blinked, surprised. "Where did you go to school?"

"I've got a Masters from UW-Lacrosse. My clinical phase was at Mayo."

He whistled softly. "When we first met, you had a part-time job at a burger place and didn't have a clue about your future."

"I always planned on college," she said simply, keeping a close eye on Cole. "I just needed to save money first."

"You never married?" The question escaped before he thought it through and he'd have done anything to snatch it back.

A long, awkward silence stretched between them.

"No," she said finally, angling a glance at him that could have sliced through steel. "Though I understand you did—your brother was more than happy to let me know that you'd gone on to far better things. Rapidly, in fact."

He felt heat crawl up his neck. After the hard life he'd led and the things he'd done for his country, he wouldn't have imagined that he was capable of such a reaction, yet here it was—heart-stopping regret, awash with embarrassment over what a fool he'd been. But he'd paid for it, in spades.

Janet had been one of the biggest mistakes of his life.

"I regret a lot of things in my life. That's one of them."

"I never asked Dee or Rob about you over the years. The subject was strictly off limits, and they knew it," she said. "But since no one is here with you, I assume the marriage didn't last."

"Never guess that every twenty-one-year-old guy is actually mature." He gave a humorless laugh. "I was lonely and impetuous. Janet worked on the base and was on the rebound. Let's just say it was not a match made in heaven. The ink was barely dry on the certificate when Janet's ex turned up and she left me."

Her gaze fixed on forest beyond the backyard, Hannah didn't answer for a long moment. "And that's what I was, too. Just a brief fling."

"No." His heart wrenched at what she believed and

what had been the truth. He'd dreamed of her for years afterward, regretting what he'd done. "You were the one who stole my heart and never gave it back."

She raised an incredulous eyebrow and snorted. "That's not how I remember things, but it's all in the past and I'm pretty sure we both dodged the proverbial bullet. All for the best."

Hannah descended the deck stairs. "Hey, kids, can you help round up these guys? C'mon, puppies— dinnertime!"

Some of the little critters followed, others went the opposite way. One black-and-white pup industriously tugged at Cole's shoelace, trying to wrestle it free. But in a few minutes they all disappeared into the garage with Cole and Hannah, where metal food dishes rattled and Cole's laughter rose above the din.

After Hannah retrieved the mixed-breed mom from a separate outside enclosure and took her to her brood, she stepped outside and started for a weathered-wood shed at the far end of the yard.

It looked like a classic, hip-roofed barn the size of a double garage, with a walk door on the side and two big, sliding barn doors at one end. A wood-fenced corral enclosed a small pasture behind it and to one side there was some sort of pen surrounded with a high chain-link fence.

"I don't suppose anyone wants to see what I've got in here?" she called over her shoulder.

Cole followed at her heels as Hannah disappeared into the shed, while Molly just hunched over her folded arms on the picnic table and made no move to follow.

Ethan strolled over to her and sat at the opposite end of the table. "So...what do you think about all of this?" he ventured after a few minutes of silence.

She lifted her gaze to the surrounding forest and scowled. "It's not Texas. And it's *cold*."

"True."

A thin whinny echoed from inside the barn. One of the sliding doors opened and Hannah emerged leading a woolly Shetland pony with Cole on top. She led the little buckskin in a slow circle then toward the picnic table.

Cole beamed. "This is Penelope. She's really old."

"She's a rescue, as well. It's probably time to hop off, but she should gain some weight in a few months and feel stronger, and after that maybe you can ride her a bit longer." Hannah reached up and helped Cole dismount before pulling a small brush from her jacket pocket. "In the meantime, you can lead her if you want and bring her carrots. She also needs to be brushed every day. Anyone here interested in doing that?"

Cole nodded, accepting the brush. He began brushing Penelope's neck. "She's pretty."

"I heard you talking to Cole in the house," Molly said to Ethan after watching her brother for a while. "And I don't get it, either."

"What's that?"

"How you could be our uncle—our *only* uncle, but we never met you. Not ever." Her mouth flattened. "Maybe we shouldn't believe you."

He considered that. "But it's true. Your dad and I were brothers. He was three years older than me. Let's see… He had a great sense of humor, he could charm his way out of trouble and he was great at every sport he tried. He had a long scar on his left inner arm from when we were playing in your great-grandfather's workshop. Did he ever tell you how it happened?"

Her lower lip trembled. "He said his brother snapped a piece of wire at him."

Typical Rob. "No. He stretched out a coiled length of wire, planning to snap it at me. But he lost his grip on one end and it zinged back. He actually had to have eight stitches."

Her brows drew together. "He had a collie. What was its name?"

"Radar." Ethan smiled. "I'm glad to see you're such a smart girl. It's good to be cautious with someone you don't know."

She turned to give him a long look. "You don't look like my dad. And—" The moment her gaze dropped to his right hand, her eyes filled with horror and she recoiled. "What is *that*?"

Cole stopped brushing the pony and craned his neck for a better view. His mouth dropped open. "Wow."

Ethan had just gotten out of Ward 57—Amputee Alley—at Walter Reed a week ago, a place where the loss of his hand and damaged leg were minor compared to so many who had lost a great deal more. Compared to the three men in his platoon who had paid the ultimate price the day of the explosion.

But seeing the kids gawk at his missing hand reminded him that he would always be different in this civilian world. And to them, he might even seem scary.

"I was in Iraq. An insurgent lobbed a grenade into the back of our transport vehicle. I lost my hand." He flexed the fingers, demonstrating the dexterity of his prosthesis. "This gives me back some of that function."

Cole's eyes rounded. "So now you're like a bionic robot guy—with superpowers?"

"Somebody has seen way too many movies," he said with what he hoped was an easy smile. "But it would be tough having just one hand and my prosthesis does help a lot."

"It…it looks like real *skin* on it," Molly whispered.

Ethan nodded. "Supposed to. But that's just a skin-colored cosmetic cover, so it doesn't draw attention. I don't always wear it."

Molly surveyed him from head to toe, her eyes filled with blatant curiosity.

"No other mechanical parts," he said, guessing at her unspoken question. "Though several bones in my right leg were shattered. I still wear a brace."

"Forever?"

He shrugged. "I hope not."

"I'm so sorry about all you've been through, Ethan," Hannah murmured. "When did it happen?"

He glanced at Molly and Cole, once again unsure of what to say in front of them. "Last spring. A couple weeks…before."

Hannah winced and closed her eyes briefly. "And that's why you couldn't come back for the funeral. I'm sorry about what I said to you earlier. I had no idea that you were injured. Cynthia should have said something to me at the funeral…or later."

"She didn't know yet. She and I were rarely in touch over the years."

Cole turned back to brushing the pony.

Molly seemed to have lost interest in the conversation, as well. She wandered along the fenced perimeter of the backyard and peered into a chain link at one end of the barn, jumping back when an explosion of black-and-white feathers flew into the air.

"That's Mabel," Hannah called out. "She's gets herself in a kerfuffle at the least thing, but Ruth and Louise are a little less silly. They're probably taking a nice sensible nap inside the barn, where it's warm."

Molly looked over her shoulder. "You rescue *chickens*?"

"A lady near town had them. When she passed away, her family brought them here. They actually do lay eggs once in a while, but not so much now that it's winter."

"Chickens. Back in Texas, I expect they would have been dinner by now," Ethan mused.

A glint of humor sparked in her eyes. "Maybe so, but I could never eat something that has a name—or such individual personalities as those hens do."

Her gaze dropped to his jeans and he realized he'd been idly massaging the deep hollow along his outer right thigh, where the explosion had ripped away most of the muscle. "Does your leg still ache a lot?"

He shrugged. "Not really."

"Right. And poor old Mabel has an IQ of two hundred."

He snorted.

"Still, I haven't noticed you limp at all."

"Only if I'm tired, or walk too far. Or," he added with a short, humorless laugh, "if I step on it wrong. Which means a return to active duty isn't yet on the horizon."

She lowered her voice. "I can only imagine how many surgeries you've been through and the months of rehab."

"I have no memory of the explosion, and very little of the month afterward. And later—with the ongoing surgeries and the intensive rehab—I wasn't able to focus on much else. I didn't look at email or snail mail for months."

She rested a gentle hand on his arm. "And no wonder. I'm so—"

"I don't want sympathy," he retorted, his voice too harsh. "I never should have—"

He stopped himself in time and looked away. Until this moment, he'd never talked about the explosion or its aftermath. Not even through his wasted months in support groups or the attempts of a private counselor. Regrets were a waste of time, because he deserved what had happened to him.

Nothing would ever change the truth of what occurred that day. And nothing could ever erase his guilt.

Chapter Three

At the sound of a car pulling to a stop outside, Hannah glanced at her watch and gave the table a final, critical glance.

Four settings of her grandmother's china were placed on the cranberry tablecloth, flanked with her own silverware, folded linen napkins and her mother's sparkly water goblets.

Warm, flaky biscuits were already nestled in a napkin-lined basket and, from the sound of approaching footsteps outside, the rest of the dinner had arrived.

She hurried to the front door and ushered in Keeley and Sophie, some of her best friends in town. The aroma of roasted turkey, buttery sage dressing and sweet potatoes flooded her senses.

She closed her eyes and inhaled. "This is incredible. I can't believe you did all of this for us!"

Keeley and Sophie set the food on the counter. "We have at least one more trip in," Sophie said with a cheerful smile as she turned for the front door. "Then we'll leave you in peace."

Ethan, seated in one of the upholstered chairs by

the fireplace, stood and turned to face them with an easy grin.

Keeley blinked and darted a quick, questioning glance at Hannah, her eyebrows raised. Sophie stumbled to a halt and simply stared.

Disconcerted, Hannah cleared her throat. "Uh, Ethan Williams, I'd like you to meet my dear friends, Keeley North and Sophie McLaren. They knew things were going to be a little crazy here and volunteered to bring Thanksgiving dinner. And, um, Keeley and Sophie, Ethan is—or was—my sister's brother-in-law. He came to see his niece and nephew."

Sophie looked as if she were on the verge of melting into a puddle of awe and admiration over the unexpected visitor.

Keeley recovered more quickly. "Nice to meet you, Ethan."

When he made no move to step closer and offer a handshake, she slid another glance at Hannah then gave him a welcoming smile. "Did you travel far?"

"I flew in from Dallas—this morning."

"Well, I'm sure the children were happy to see you," Keeley murmured. "As you'll see, we brought way, way too much food, and I hope you'll all enjoy it."

Sophie finally found her voice. "I've been dying to meet the kids. Where are they?"

Hannah tipped her head toward the bedrooms. "Just hold on a minute."

"We'll go ahead and finish bringing in the food."

Ethan followed the two women outside to help, and soon containers of mashed potatoes and gravy, green bean casserole and three pies filled the counter.

Molly edged to the threshold of her room and glanced

at the newcomers, then bowed her head, but Hannah had to go into Cole's bedroom to convince him to come out.

Keeley beamed at them both. "I am so happy to meet you two. Molly and Cole, right? I hope we'll get to see a lot of you around town."

"I hope so, too," Sophie echoed. "My son Eli is in fourth grade, and I know he'll be very excited about meeting you both."

"Tell Hannah to bring you by my shop anytime," Keeley added. "I always have fresh homemade cookies for special visitors."

Hannah glanced between them. "Can you join us for dinner? It would only take a moment to add some place settings."

"Wish I could," Sophie said with a wistful smile. "We have a lot of catching up to do. But Josh is on call at the ER today, so I need to be home with Eli."

"And I need to get back to my store. The day after Thanksgiving is usually really busy. But I hope you'll all enjoy the meal."

Hannah walked them out to Keeley's SUV. "This was so kind of you—going to all this work. I can't thank you enough. I know the kids missed having their Thanksgiving dinner yesterday."

"Poor kids," Sophie said in a somber tone. "I can't imagine how tough this year has been for them. And what's with the uncle? The kids were down in Texas and got on their plane just yesterday, yet he's already made a trip from Dallas up here? What's really going on?"

Hannah darted a look back at the house. "It's…a long story, but basically he says he wants custody."

Keeley gasped. "Isn't it a little late?"

"And what about the kids—uprooted then being

hauled right back?" Sophie chimed in. "That's just not right."

"I agree. Totally. And I plan to fight him every step of the way, if it comes to that. But he is their uncle, so I can hardly shove him out the door…at least not yet."

Sophie's eyes widened. "You're going to let him stay here?"

"We haven't discussed how long he'll be in Wisconsin or where he'll stay. I hope he'll be leaving in a day or so. But, no, I don't think it's appropriate for him to stay here. I don't have an empty guest room now, anyway."

Keeley gently gripped Hannah's forearm. "You'd better get back inside before the food goes cold. But call me—day or night—if you need help or just need to talk. Okay?"

"And me, too," Sophie whispered. "This place is so isolated, now I'll wonder if you're even safe here."

Hannah smiled at them both. "I taught personal safety classes at the community college for four years, remember? And I have 9-1-1 on speed dial. We'll be fine."

But as she watched them drive away, Ethan's words slipped into her thoughts.

He'd mentioned an explosion.

She shivered, imagining all he'd gone through. The pain. The loss of a limb and thus the loss of his life as he'd known it. The surgeries and long, painful therapy. Probably even PTSD.

Given his proximity to that explosion and the extent of his physical damage, had he also suffered a TBI—traumatic brain injury? Unfortunately it was all too likely.

A soldier could fully recover from a TBI…or face disabling symptoms for a lifetime.

During the clinical phase of her physician's assistant program she'd seen one such problem firsthand when a vet with severe mood swings sent an orderly to the floor at her feet, out cold.

Ethan had the right to his privacy, but she needed to keep two young children safe. So she would keep on her guard. Watch him carefully. And she would talk to him privately when the moment seemed right.

But in the meantime, she would also keep her cell close at hand.

Ethan watched the kids as they sat at the table pushing bits of turkey around their plates, their eyes downcast. Neither had eaten enough to keep a sparrow alive.

Were they remembering Thanksgiving dinners from years past, when their family was still complete? How could that grief and loss ever be repaired?

"This is the best meal I've had in a dozen years," he said reverently into the strained silence as he forked up another bite of mashed potatoes and rich gravy. "Everything is delicious."

Molly looked up from sculpting a mountain range with her potatoes and frowned at him. "A dozen years. Really?"

He nodded. "I've been stationed in various places overseas all that time and almost never made it back for a Thanksgiving dinner in the States. Your aunt Hannah has some mighty nice friends to go to all this effort for you."

Tears started down Cole's face. Hannah moved to his side and wrapped him in a gentle embrace. "I know coming here is a big change, after all those months at Aunt Cynthia's. And I know how tough it is, honey."

Had Ethan's words about home-cooked meals reminded him of his mom? Cole's thin shoulders shook and his tears flowed faster. "I…I just want my m-mom back," he whispered brokenly. "A-and my dad."

"I know you do, sweetheart. I miss your mom a lot, too. And I know that right now you both feel hopeless and overwhelmed." Hannah gently rubbed his back. "You'll never forget your parents and you'll never stop loving them. But in time, I promise it will become easier."

Molly fixed her gaze on her brother, her lower lip trembling. She abruptly pushed away from the table and fled to her room, slamming the door behind her.

Ethan had led men into battle. He'd faced off against the enemy too many times to count. But now he stared after the girl with a searing sense of helplessness. "Should I go after her?" he asked finally.

"Not just yet. Give her some time."

Cole pulled away from Hannah's embrace and slouched lower in his chair, draping an arm over Maisie. The old dog hadn't moved from his side since they'd all sat for dinner and now she sidled even closer to rest her head on his lap. "Can I go to my room?"

"Would you like some pie first?" Hannah ruffled his hair. "Sophie brought pumpkin, cherry and a French silk—that's like a creamy chocolate pudding. Or, I have chocolate chip ice cream."

"No thanks."

Ethan watched the boy trudge away, the retriever at his side, then stood to help Hannah clear the plates and serving dishes. "I wish there was something I could do, right now, to make them happy."

"What it will take is prayer and love, and lots of time. But time is elusive, because it's all so relative. Now they're going through this year of firsts—the grief

of birthdays and holidays without their mom and dad."
Hannah began emptying the leftovers into plastic containers and loading the serving dishes and glassware
into the dishwasher. "They will adjust, but every big life
event will bring it all back. Confirmation. Graduation.
Weddings. It just goes on, because they'll wish they still
had their parents to share those times. But you know all
that—Rob said you two lost your mom early, right?"

"She walked out on us when we were in grade school
and we only saw her once after that. She moved to
Maine, remarried, then died at thirty-five. Jay-walking,
of all things."

"But your grandpa raised you, correct? Rob used
to say he was quite a pistol—and the grumpiest person he'd ever met." She looked over her shoulder while
stowing the leftovers in the refrigerator. "It must not
have been easy for you boys."

"One way to put it, I guess."

After living with a single father who'd had a short
temper, little interest in parenthood and a career involving a lot of travel, the parade of live-in babysitters
had finally ended when Dad ditched Rob and Ethan at
their grandfather's house. Ethan could still hear Dad
yelling that he couldn't cope with them any longer and
he wasn't going to try.

"I'm so sorry," Hannah murmured as she began filling the sink with hot, sudsy water.

He shrugged. "My parents never should have married
each other, and having two kids couldn't cement bonds
that didn't exist. But I guess these things happen." He
eyed the flatware and the stack of plates. "Can those
go in the dishwasher?"

"Not the good china or silverware."

"Do you want me to wash or dry?"

She glanced at the oversize clock above the sink. "Thanks, but it'll take just a minute to wash these few things and I'll let it all air-dry. Anyway, it's already getting dark. Are you heading into town for the night? Or the airport?"

"Town."

She washed and rinsed a plate and gently rested it in the drying rack, then took a deep breath and turned to face him. "And then what? Do you have any plans?"

When he'd talked to one of his aunt's attorneys in Dallas and insisted that he wanted to pursue custody, she'd confirmed what Hannah had told him earlier today. There would be monthly visits by a caseworker to see how well the children were adapting to Hannah and their new home before permanent custody would be granted—probably after ninety days if all the reports were good.

She'd also warned him that he could petition for custody, but if the children were well settled and content in their new home, it was unlikely that the court would agree to any further disruption of their lives.

But it was the attorney's additional words that kept playing through Ethan's thoughts.

The situation would be evaluated—especially regarding how well the children were bonding—and with whom. Which led him to believe that he still had a chance.

He was a stranger to them, so that was now a moot point. But the attorney had suggested he spend as much time as possible with the children—without upsetting them or challenging Hannah in any way—prior to the first thirty-day custody evaluation.

If he wanted any chance at all, the children needed to be comfortable with him, and want to join him in Texas.

Hannah looked at him expectantly, clearly waiting for an answer.

"I'm staying in town, at least until Christmas."

Her jaw dropped. "In Aspen Creek? Don't you have a home in Dallas...or somewhere?"

"Just a condo—but it's always been more of a storage unit than a place to live." He shrugged. "Right now I'm on medical leave, so there's no place I need to be. A month or so here would be as good as any place else."

"To do what? Have...a...a vacation?"

"Of sorts."

Her face pale, she fidgeted with the dishcloth, wiping at the already spotless kitchen counter. "You have a place to stay?"

"Reservations at a B and B on this side of town that also has some year-round cabins. I haven't checked in yet, but the off-season rate was better than any of the other places I found online."

"Y-you arranged all of this before even flying north?" She worried her bottom lip with her teeth. "What else have you planned?"

"I want to spend time with my niece and nephew."

"Now—when they've barely arrived here? Is that fair to them?"

"It's time I got to know them—something I failed to do before. As their uncle, I understand I have that right, but I won't interfere."

"But they'll be in school starting this Monday, up through December twenty-third." Her voice took on a desperate note. "They'll be in school all day. They'll have homework and will be spending time with kids they're going to meet at church and school..."

"Understood, but surely I can see them now and then.

Isn't it good for them to know more about what little family they have left? I promise I won't be in the way."

"Not much," she muttered under her breath. "Why not come later, when they've had a chance to get settled? Maybe Easter."

"Rob and I had a childhood filled with acrimony and irresponsible adults who didn't much care about us. That isn't going to happen to Molly and Cole."

"There will be no such acrimony and lack of responsibility here, I assure you. I love these kids."

Love? Maybe. But he knew all too well how flighty and irresponsible she could be, and he wasn't going to take any chances. "I need to make sure my brother's children have a much better life than he and I did. I owe him this much."

She sagged against the counter and he could see the realization dawning in her eyes. "Which means you *are* serious about wanting custody. This trip is all about you trying to win them over before permanent custody is finalized."

"I want what's best for them, Hannah. A loving, stable home, in a familiar place. Except for their dad's misguided move to Oklahoma last year for another job that didn't pan out, they have always lived in Texas."

"A nice sentiment. But will you really follow through— or will you lose interest and foist them off on some nanny when you go overseas again? You did say that your return to active duty isn't yet on the horizon, so you obviously hope to leave again." She blew out a slow breath. "I don't mean to keep bringing up the past, but I seem to recall that your good intentions don't always amount to much. You once made some very serious promises to me."

"A whirlwind romance when we were too young to know better."

"You were already in the service, which implies responsibility and honor to me. You made promises and then you not only reneged on them but you disappeared without a word. Without an apology. Without explanation. Not even a goodbye. I was packed, ready and excited, Ethan. And you left me standing on the courthouse steps. *Alone.*"

"There's nothing I can do to change that now. I only wish it was possible to make up for what I did."

She gave a short laugh. "Not necessary. Eventually I realized two things—that I was lucky to have escaped marriage to a man I couldn't trust. And, I escaped repeating history."

"History?"

"My dad was military, as you might remember," she said bitterly. "He ran our home like a barracks, and woe to anyone who challenged his authority or failed to measure up. But he'd always promised to come home—no matter where he was sent or what he did." She turned away.

"But he couldn't keep that promise?" Ethan asked gently.

"A new recruit went crazy on the base one nice, sunny day. Shot Dad six times in the chest while shouting nonsense about war and the evil army officer who was sending him home. I was just twelve, visiting Dad's office on Career Day. I saw him die. I thought I would be next. But then his killer turned the gun on himself. The whole floor was awash in blood and I was too scared and shocked to even move."

"I'm so sorry, Hannah."

"I swore then that I wanted nothing more to do with

military life when I grew up. Living with Dad had been tough, but seeing him die because he wore a uniform was a thousand times worse. Military families are amazing, strong people, and we all owe them so much for what they sacrifice every day. But I'm just not that strong—and I could never handle that life again."

He'd seen the horrors of war for over a decade. Dealt with his nightmares as best he could. But he could not imagine what that terrible day had done to an innocent child.

"So you see," she added softly, "you jilted me. You made me a laughingstock in town. But you also saved me from a life of living with my worst fears. I won't ever trust you again on any count, but I guess I also owe you my thanks."

Chapter Four

"So this is downtown Aspen Creek, guys. All of the shop owners have been decorating for this weekend, and the Christmas Committee has been putting up decorations in the town square." Hannah parked at the north end of Main Street in front of the shoe store and looked over her shoulder. "Next, I want to buy winter boots for you both, then we'll walk down to the square so you can see the crew decorating the pine trees. If you aren't too tired after supper, we can come back for the lighting ceremony and a sleigh ride."

Cole perked up at that. "With horses?"

"Yes, indeed." She grinned at Cole and his sister, happy that her plans for the day seemed to be working out. An introduction to the festive downtown area, a yummy lunch somewhere and then maybe a movie might be a good start at helping the two kids feel at home. She hoped. And surely they'd enjoy the Christmas lights and carolers tonight—Aspen Creek's kick-off weekend for the holidays.

"A stable near town always brings a pair of dappled gray Percherons and a beautiful sleigh for evening sleigh rides," she continued. "They're here Saturdays and Sundays during the Christmas season. I love hearing those heavy brass jingle bells coming down the street."

Cole unbuckled his seat belt and leaned forward. "Can we go more than once?"

"Of course we can."

Molly directed a disinterested glance out the window, then picked at the snowflake design on her new wool mittens. "Can't have a sleigh. No snow."

Hannah laughed. "You're right about that. When there isn't any snow, they bring a pretty carriage with a fringed roof and big wooden wheels with red and white spokes. If the weather forecast holds, we might have enough for a real sleigh for tomorrow."

Her cell phone chirped and she grabbed it out of her purse. Her happy mood vanished. *Ethan.* She hesitated then took the call with a resigned sigh. "Yes?"

"You mentioned going into town today. Can I treat you all to lunch somewhere?"

She glanced at her watch. She'd gone through the children's clothing boxes this morning to check on what they needed for the colder climate and then she'd taken the kids shopping. After an hour at the Children's Shoppe, both of them now had extra sweatshirts and warm pullover sweaters, goose-down jackets and snow pants in their favorite colors, with mittens to match.

But she still needed to buy them snow boots and sleds, and take them down to the town square. If there was enough time, they could also drop in on Keeley's antiques store for cookies.

And—admittedly—stop somewhere for lunch. "I... guess so. In an hour?"

"Perfect. Do you have a favorite place?"

Despite her resolutions regarding Ethan, the deep

timbre of his voice still sent an unwanted tingle of awareness shivering over her skin.

"I think the kids would like the Creek Malt Shop. It's fairly new, but has 1950s décor, and they make malts with scoops of real ice cream. Their burgers are the best in town and they have old-fashioned pinball machines in the back—no charge." She glanced at the kids. "What do you two think—sound good?"

When they nodded, she returned to the call. "The Malt Shop faces the town square. We were heading down there to see the holiday decorations after we finish shopping, anyway. We'll be there in an hour."

She ended the call and sighed. They would show up to meet him, but she doubted she could eat a single bite. Her stomach was already tying itself into a tight knot.

She'd stayed awake until two in the morning, worrying about what the future would bring with Ethan in the mix. Praying that he might see the flaws in his plan and just give up and go back to Dallas.

But, nope—he was still here. And he was already finding ways to keep in touch.

Which proved that she'd better plan to keep on her toes.

Ethan idly ran a fingertip through the condensation on his malt glass and settled back in the booth. He glanced at his watch once more.

The hesitance in Hannah's voice had been unmistakable over the phone. Would she even show up?

His booth was right in front of a plateglass window looking out over the street and, beyond that, the town square where clusters of folks were busy winding strands of Christmas lights on the dozen pine trees scattered throughout the little park.

A larger team was tackling the towering blue spruce in the center, utilizing a cherry picker to reach the very top.

Though it was only the Saturday after Thanksgiving Day, Christmas music already blared from loudspeakers in the square, and even through the window, he could hear the banter and laughter from the crowd as they worked.

Christmas seemed to be everywhere.

Even in this hamburger joint, there had to be a dozen tabletop-sizes Christmas trees with twinkly lights perched on shelves, counters and in the corners. Wreaths and Christmas stockings hung on the walls. Over each booth and table a sprig of mistletoe hung from the ceiling on a bright red ribbon.

It was as if Christmas had exploded in here, and it made him edgy. *Bah humbug.*

He caught sight of Hannah—her shimmering, pale blond hair unmistakable, even from a distance—weaving through the crowd across the street, where she was making slow progress by chatting to every person she met. Cole walked at her side, wearing a puffy, bright red jacket. Molly, in a similar hot-pink jacket, followed a few yards behind with a sullen expression.

They finally made their way across the street and he saw Hannah square her shoulders and take a deep breath before ushering the kids inside the Malt Shop. From her grim expression she didn't seem at all happy to be there.

In a moment they arrived at his booth. Molly and Hannah slid in opposite him and Cole scrambled next to Ethan. The faint, familiar scent of Hannah's perfume wafted in the air, reminding him of the past they'd shared. One he needed to forget.

"Sorry if we're a bit late," Hannah murmured as she grabbed menus from the rack behind the napkin dispenser and dealt them out.

"I got a new coat and mittens and boots," Cole announced. "And other stuff, 'cause it's cold here."

Molly rolled her eyes and dropped her gaze to her menu.

"Looks like you got a new coat, as well," Ethan said to her. "Have you found your sleds yet?"

She shook her head.

"We never had sleds before," Cole announced. "'Cause we didn't get enough snow. But Aunt Hannah says we'll get *lots* tonight. Five whole inches!"

"The most I ever saw in Dallas was a few flurries." Ethan shifted his gaze to Hannah. "So I've never gone shopping for sleds, either. Can I come along?"

She gave him a stiff smile. "Of course. The hardware store is a couple of blocks over and it usually has a good supply."

Cole's eyes lit up. "Maybe you can both get a sled, too, and then we can all go. Aunt Hannah says she'll bring hot cocoa and marshmallows and cookies. So we have *lots* of energy."

Ethan chuckled. "Somehow I don't think you'll run out of that anytime soon."

"But you'll come sledding, right? And for the carriage ride tonight?"

"Well…" He angled another glance up at Hannah. "Is that all right with you?"

The corner of her eye twitched but she nodded. "Aspen Creek Park is just a mile north of town and there are good sliding hills near the campground. The snowplows don't usually clear the country roads before the afternoon on Sundays, though. So…" She considered for a moment. "Maybe two o'clock tomorrow?"

"Deal."

"And the carriage ride, too?" Cole insisted.

A waitress in a red-striped uniform appeared at the table with a tray of water glasses and a smile. "As you can see, we're kinda busy, so just wave to me when you're ready to order."

"I want a cheeseburger and a chocolate malt, with French fries," Cole announced instantly.

"Same," Molly muttered.

"That didn't take long. Hot-fudge shake and a grilled chicken sandwich for me," Hannah said without looking at her menu. "Ethan?"

"Cheeseburger and fries. I've already got my malt."

Molly eyed the colorful flashing lights on the pinball machines at the back and gave the waitress a pleading look. "Can we play?"

"Sure. Nice change from all those computer games, if you ask me. Unless someone else comes in and wants a turn, you can play as long as you like." The waitress grinned. "At least, until your food comes. I'm sure your parents can keep an eye on you from right here."

Hannah's gaze flew to Molly—expecting a meltdown over the waitress's assumption. But the kids launched out of the booth and made a beeline for the bank of pinball machines without a backward glance.

"Whew," she whispered, her hands clenched on the tabletop. "That was close. I'm finding casual conversations can be quite a minefield with people who aren't yet aware of our circumstances. I'm sure the word is spreading, but still…"

It would probably be the same in Texas, Ethan realized, though he couldn't help but think it would be easier if the kids were at least on their home turf. And come to think of it, there would be a few people who could make assumptions. He didn't know people there anymore except Cynthia and his dad. He'd been gone all of his adult life.

"I know this will be a hard Christmas for the kids, with their parents gone. It's going to bring back so many memories of the happier times." Hannah twisted in her seat for a better view of the pinball machines. "But Christmas is my favorite time of year, and I'm excited about sharing the whole Aspen Creek holiday experience with them. I hope they'll have some good times, anyway. Maybe make some new memories. This town is amazing from now until the last day of December."

"What makes it so special?"

"A quaint little tourist town like Aspen Creek really celebrates. Lighted wreaths on all of the old-fashioned lampposts, twinkling lights everywhere, and the festivities go on and on. Carolers. Games. A skating rink in the town square. A lighting ceremony there this evening. We draw large crowds of weekend shoppers from the Twin Cities and Chicago because of it. I love the horse-drawn sleigh rides in town on weekend evenings, and our Christmas Eve candlelight service at the Aspen Creek Community Church is always beyond beautiful. I just hope the kids will enjoy it all."

She'd come into the café looking tense, but now her eyes sparkled and she gave him her first real smile. The sheer strength of it sent a jolt straight to his chest. "I suppose they will."

"Sorry." She gave a quick, self-conscious laugh. "You look a little stunned, but when I get started on Christmas in Aspen Creek, I start to babble. My friends tease me about being one of Santa's elves."

Hearing her love of Christmas touched a hollow place in his heart. Made him wish he could attend every event and try to absorb some of the joy she radiated, and awaken in himself some measure of Christmas spirit.

But Christmas stirred no happy memories. It was fraught with a lifetime of disappointment—failed wishes and lost dreams. It was something to get past, to forget. There'd been no Norman Rockwell holidays in his childhood and none later, either.

And, right now, all of these local festivities carried a great deal of risk to his plans. Would the kids become so enthralled by Hannah's joy and this fairy tale of a town that they wouldn't want to move back to Dallas with him?

He listened to the bells and chimes of the antique pinball machines at the back of the café and watched the kids' rapt attention as the pretty lights flashed.

And once again he kicked himself for not getting back to Dallas sooner. No matter what his doctors and therapists had said, he should've toughed it out on his own without those last months of therapy.

Then he would have been home before Cynthia's injury and could've picked up Molly and Cole before Hannah whisked them off to Wisconsin.

Where there were puppies and ponies and dazzling Christmas events that might make them want to stay with her for good.

Chapter Five

Hannah looped an arm around Molly's and Cole's shoulders and gathered them close for a hug as more people arrived in the town square for the lighting ceremony.

Darkness had fallen while she was doing the animal chores back home and now light snow was drifting downward in gentle swirls to frost the pine trees and sparkle on the children's stocking caps and jackets.

With no wind and the temp hovering just below freezing, it would be relatively comfortable out here for the hour-long program, but maybe her little Texans weren't accustomed enough to the cold. "Be sure to tell me if you're getting chilly, okay? We can go home whenever you want."

"I want a sleigh ride for *sure*." Cole tipped his head back to catch snowflakes on his tongue, and even Molly joined in.

"The church is selling hot chocolate and Christmas cookies, so if you—"

"Yes!" Cole exclaimed, tugging on the hem of her yellow ski jacket. "Please?"

Nodding to people she knew from church or the

clinic, Hannah led the kids to the food stand at the other side of the square. Painted white with green vertical stripes, its red canvas roof was strung with icicle lights.

Inside, Beth Stone and Olivia Lawson, two of Hannah's friends from the local book club, were dressed in Mrs. Santa caps and white wigs. Over their winter coats they wore aprons adorned with jingle bells and giant neck-to-knee Christmas trees bedecked with flashing lights.

Both of them beamed when Hannah finally reached the head of the line. Cole looked up at their outfits in confusion. "There are two Mrs. Santas?"

"We're just her helpers for today," Olivia assured him with a kindly smile. "She's very busy this time of year."

"Keeley told us about you two," Beth said with a warm smile as she handed Molly and Cole gingerbread men and hot chocolate topped with pastel marshmallows. "We're both so happy to meet you!"

"Thanks," Molly mumbled. Cole shyly nodded.

"Love those aprons," Hannah teased as she handed over a ten dollar bill. "They're just so understated."

Beth laughed. "We're good until the AA batteries wear down. If you really like them, I stocked some extras in the gift area of my bookstore."

Olivia, an elegant and slender woman of seventy, craned her neck to search the nearby crowd. "So where's this Texas cowboy of yours? Keeley tells me he's quite a hunk."

"A what?" The term was so unexpected from a sophisticated, reserved woman like Olivia that Hannah sputtered on her first sip of cocoa, laughing.

And just then she felt the back of her neck start to burn and knew that, without a doubt, the hunk had to be standing right behind her. Embarrassment flooded her cheeks with heat.

"Hey, kids. Hannah." His voice rumbled against her ear.

Mortified, she froze for a moment. Had it sounded like she was laughing at him?

Cole turned around and, bless his heart, broke the awkward silence. "We dint know you're a cowboy, Uncle Ethan," he breathed in awe. "That's even better than a soldier 'cause you get to have horses *and* a gun."

"He's not a cowboy, stupid," Molly said, elbowing him and sending his cup of hot cocoa sloshing dangerously. But then she looked up at Ethan and frowned. "Are you?"

"Nope. Your aunt Hannah is closer to that than I am. She's got the horse."

Surprised at his gracious reply, Hannah felt even more awkward about her inadvertent insult.

Molly rolled her eyes. "Penelope isn't any bigger than I am."

He lifted a shoulder and smiled at her. "Maybe the next one will be taller. But if you want to see something big, wait until you see the team headed this way."

"Where? Can we go now?" Cole spun around, trying to peer through the crowd milling in the square. This time his hot chocolate spilled over his mitten and onto his new snow boots.

Panic flooded into his face and he jerked back, his lower lip trembling. "Sorry. I'm really sorry, Hannah."

The ramifications of his fearful reaction sent a chill through Hannah. She met Ethan's gaze and frowned, then bent to Cole's level. "It's only a cup of cocoa, sweetie. No big deal. I'll get you a refill."

He stared helplessly at her, like a rabbit caught in a trap, his eyes sheened with unshed tears.

"Really, it's not a problem, kiddo," she said with a smile. She gave him a hug. "And we will go see the horses when they start giving rides after the program. Promise."

Keeley silently telegraphed unspoken concern as she leaned over the counter to hand Hannah a new cup of cocoa. Hannah shook her head slowly in return before shepherding the children toward the benches set up in the middle of the square.

The thought of a sweet little six-year-old boy fearing punishment made her heart clench.

Someone had been severe with the poor little guy. His father? A former babysitter? *Cynthia?* None of them would be in his life again, but this was yet one more subject to bring up gently with him when the time was right.

She sat on a bench toward the back of the crowd with Molly and Cole on either side of her. Ethan sat next to Cole and draped an arm over his thin shoulders.

"Hey, buddy, I hear there's going to be lots of snow for sledding tomorrow. Are you excited about using your new sled?"

Cole nodded, his head bowed.

"I wonder which one will be the fastest," Ethan mused. "I've never had a sled before, so this will be really fun."

Cole gave him a sideways glance. "Never?"

"Nope. And I've never ice-skated, either. I noticed an ice rink on the other side of the square, so maybe that's something we could all do, too."

"Molly and me don't have skates."

"I'll bet we can work something out. When we were

at the hardware store for the sleds, I noticed that they have a used skate exchange. Good idea for kids who are always growing, right?" He leaned forward to catch Molly's eye. "What about you? I can see you now—spinning on your skates like a ballerina. Would you like that?"

Molly shrugged and plopped back in her seat, though maybe there'd been the faintest glimmer of interest in her eyes.

The mayor stood at the podium, tapped the microphone and wished everyone a happy Christmas season, then stepped aside. A dozen carolers wearing Santa hats took his place and began singing Christmas carols and hymns, encouraging everyone to sing along.

The beauty of this night, with snowflakes falling and her sister's two children at her side, filled Hannah with love and gratitude. When Cole reached over to hold her hand, she felt overwhelmed by her many blessings.

She lifted her eyes skyward. *Dee, I promise that your children will be safe and loved, and I'll do everything in my power to raise them as you wanted to.*

As the sweet strains of "Silent Night" drifted off into the night, the mayor stepped back up to the podium and shouted, "Merry Christmas!"

With a flip of a switch, all of the trees on the square blazed with light. The tallest, a massive old blue spruce towering thirty feet into the sky, sparkled with thousands of tiny white lights.

"Wow," Molly breathed. "It's so pretty here! Like a fairy land."

Hannah gave her a one-armed hug. "I know. I come every year and I never get tired of it. These gorgeous lights will be on until New Year's Day."

Cole tugged on her jacket. "Can we go see the horses

now? What if there's a big line and we can't have a ride?"

"Problem solved. People used to get cold waiting in line, so the town council decided to sell advance tickets for various time slots. I bought ours this morning on-line." Hannah reached into her jacket pocket and pulled out an envelope. "People can still line up for any empty seats, but this way we don't have to wait. All four of us—you, too, Ethan—need to be on the other side of the square in ten minutes."

Cole and Molly darted ahead. Ethan fell into step with Hannah, both keeping an eye on the kids.

A dusting of snow sparkled in Ethan's raven hair and on the shoulders of his navy jacket. She suppressed the impulse to brush away the snow and jammed her hands into her pockets. "So, what did you think?"

He angled a glance at her as they strode after the kids. "Nice evening."

"Just nice? I thought it was beautiful. All of the carolers, the moment the town square was lit up and—look down the street—all of the wreaths on the streetlamps are now lit up, as well. And check out the lovely shop windows. The town has a contest every year for those displays. I just can't get enough of it all."

He chuckled at that. "I can tell."

She frowned, thinking over the day. "You didn't need to buy four sleds, you know. I hope you didn't feel obligated when Cole went crazy over all those choices. I can certainly pay you back."

He looked affronted. "No. Actually, while I'm here, I'd like to help with their expenses. It seems only fair. You must have spent a lot on the winter clothes you bought them today."

Hannah felt her hackles rise. "Not necessary. It was

fun getting them outfitted with some of the things they'll need here."

Just ahead, Molly and Cole stopped along the sidewalk where two massive grays, in gleaming black leather and silver harnesses, stood patiently. One shook its head, sending the bells on its harness jingling.

Cole danced excitedly. "Just look at the horses, Aunt Hannah. They're pretty! And look at the carriage—it has ribbons and bells and Christmas lights!"

Hannah approached the driver, who was dressed in a Santa suit and already calling for those with tickets for the first trip, and then motioned to Ethan and the children. "This is it—our scheduled ride. Climb aboard!"

There were two rows of bench seats behind the raised front seat for the driver. Cole and Molly sat in middle with two other children who were already on board. Ethan and Hannah ended up in the back, wedged together by another seated couple.

Hannah tried to scoot over to avoid being pressed so tightly against Ethan, but to no avail. "I'm sorry," she whispered.

"No problem." He lifted an arm and curved it around her shoulders, which gave them both a bit more room. "Seems like old times—in my old Chevy truck."

He remembered that?

From the moment he'd appeared at her door she'd been wary of him, suspicious of his motives and worried about the possibility of a looming legal battle over the children's future. She'd carefully ignored his physical appeal—he was simply a tall, incredibly good-looking guy, nothing more. But that hadn't been difficult. She'd only had to recall her hurt and anger at the callous way she'd been jilted—and his brother's cruel words afterward—to put that foolishness to rest.

But now, sitting so close to him, feeling the warmth of his leg against her jeans and his hard-muscled body pressed against hers, she could sense his strength even through the layers of their jackets. He made her feel safe. Protected.

Which made no sense since she knew she couldn't trust him one bit. Not when something really counted.

The carriage dipped to one side as the driver lumbered up onto his seat and then twisted around to doff his cap in greeting. "Well, folks, happy holidays to you all! I'm Pete. Frank and Earl here have been pulling this carriage for five years, so we should have a good, steady ride for the next half hour. Grab the folded lap robes stored under your seats if you get cold. Any questions before we start?"

Molly raised a timid hand. "Can you ride these horses?"

Pete chuckled. "Sure. Some folks ride draft horses, but I've gotten old and prefer driving. Creaky bones, I guess."

He shook out some slack in the reins and clucked at the team. They dutifully plodded forward, the bells on their harnesses rhythmically jingling, the leather creaking.

The carriage swayed as the horses clopped down Main Street beneath the swags of Christmas lights suspended across the street between lampposts.

"This is just lovely," Hannah murmured, glancing up at Ethan.

The rhythmic hoof beats, the warm scent of the horses and the aroma of the surrounding pine forest were almost mesmerizing.

The strong line of his jaw and his five-o'clock shadow were more than a little mesmerizing, too.

She pulled her gaze away and leaned forward. "Look to the left, kids. See that antiques and gift shop with the icicle lights hanging in the windows? It belongs to Keeley, who helped bring us Thanksgiving dinner yesterday. We ran out of time today, but we'll stop by another day. She wants you to try her yummy cookies."

Cole turned around. "She's nice."

Guessing at his thoughts, she smiled. "You'll both have lots of friends here, soon. I promise. You'll get to meet lots of kids at church tomorrow, and on Monday you'll see them in school, too."

"I don't want to go to school. Or church, either," Molly muttered without turning around. "I won't know *anybody*."

The girl next to her had been staring at the Christmas lights and bickering with her brother. But now she angled a curious look at Molly. "What grade are you in?"

"Sixth."

"I'm in eighth. But my cousin Joanie is in sixth." The girl shuddered. "I hope you don't get Mrs. Stone for math. I heard she's tough."

Molly shot a desperate glance at Hannah. "Did I? I *hate* math."

"You're all set to start, but I don't remember everything on the class schedule they sent me. Except that you got Mrs. Fisher for English. She goes to my church and is really nice, I promise. We can check the schedule when we get home."

Molly bowed her head. "It's dumb to change schools now, after everybody has already made friends. I'll never catch up, anyway. Everything will be different and I'll look stupid."

"Well, I'm Faith, and you know me. And I'll tell Joanie you're really cool, so then you'll know her.

She's cool, too." The other girl gave her a gentle, teasing shoulder bump. "And you aren't the only new one at school. We got two new kids in my classes just last week. Anyway, Christmas vacation comes up soon and after that it's like we're all starting new."

Molly shot her a grateful look then settled back in her seat.

"Thank goodness for small favors," Hannah said under her breath. "Monday might not be so hard, after all."

Chapter Six

The next morning Cole and Molly stood at the living room windows in their new flannel pajamas and stared out at the winter wonderland of white in awe.

"This is more than five inches," Molly whispered. "It has to be."

Hannah laughed. "A good foot so far. The new forecast predicts about fifteen inches with a possibility of forty-mile-an-hour wind gusts. So what do you think of all this?"

"Does this mean school will be canceled tomorrow?" The desperate note of hope in Molly's voice was unmistakable. "We never got anything like this in Dallas."

"I can't say what will happen with school. We'll listen to the radio or check the internet for closing announcements. But don't forget Faith and her cousin Joanie. You'll have two friends right at the start."

Molly shot a glum look at her. "I don't even know what Joanie looks like."

"After the carriage ride yesterday I started thinking, and I believe that family may have just started attending my church. So if the plow comes in time—which I doubt—we could go into town for the service and you'd probably get to meet Joanie and some of the other kids, too. Wouldn't that be great?"

Molly plopped into one of the upholstered chairs, her legs dangling over the armrest. "I guess."

"That was one of my goals for today, anyhow. Another was to make sure we had fun sledding." She shook her head. "But Old Man Winter sure isn't cooperating. And though I know you don't want to hear it, I want to make sure you both are all set for school tomorrow."

"What about my class schedule?"

"I've got it right there on the counter, next to the phone."

Molly hurried to get it. Squeezed her eyes tight. Then slowly unfolded the letter. "Mrs. Fisher…Miss Hayward…Mr. Coe…Mrs. Belkin…" She fell silent for a long moment then slapped the schedule onto the counter. "And Mrs. Stone. Math. I knew I wouldn't be lucky, I just *knew* it," she wailed. "I'm bad at math, so of *course* I got the mean one. I'm going to fail."

"You heard the opinion of just one student," Hannah said mildly. "And Faith didn't even have that teacher. Secondhand information isn't always right. Maybe Faith's friend was a slacker who didn't do his or her homework."

"Or maybe she tried super hard and the teacher failed her just out of spite," Molly retorted.

"I don't imagine that will happen. Anyway, math isn't subjective. Your answers are either right or wrong. But I can promise you that whatever happens, I will help. Okay?"

"Can we go sledding right now?" Cole looked up from pressing his fingertips against the frosted edges of the windowpanes, his eyes bright with excitement and anticipation. "You got us boots and snow pants."

"You're definitely all set, but there aren't good slid-ing hills nearby—the forest is too dense. We'll need to drive down to Aspen Creek Park for that—but not in this weather."

Cole's face fell. "Can't we try?"

"We have to wait for the snowplow. I can't prom-ise when he'll come—especially if the wind picks up. Blowing and drifting can be a real problem out here, so sometimes the county pulls the plows off the road. Then we just have to wait."

"But you have a big car. I bet it could go."

"Even if my SUV could make it, it's not worth taking any chances. We might get there but not make it back today, and who would feed all the animals?"

"Does that mean Uncle Ethan can't get here, either?"

The ceiling lights in the kitchen flickered ominously and Molly's eyes rounded. "What was that?"

"No worries. Sometimes the power goes out during storms if a line goes down somewhere. We usually get it back within a few hours."

"So in the meantime we could freeze to death, right? And not be found till spring?"

Hannah smothered a smile at Molly's dramatics. "Not a chance. We have the wood-burning fireplace, plus I have lots of candles, flashlights and several ker-osene lamps, so we won't be sitting in the dark. I also have a generator to keep just the essentials going." Han-nah moved to the fireplace and opened the glass doors. "In fact, I think a little fire would be cheery right now, don't you?"

Cole followed her. "Can I help?"

Hannah sat on the raised hearth and pointed to the alcove next to the fireplace. "Can you hand me some good pieces of firewood? Four or five should be plenty right now."

Reaching inside the firebox, she opened the damper then helped him arrange the wood and tinder. She struck the match and in a few minutes the sweet scent of burning pine wafted into the air.

As warmth began to radiate into the room, Maisie, Bootsie and all three cats claimed spots right in front of the fire.

She dusted off her hands. "Great job. Thanks, Cole. Now, who wants to help make chocolate chip cookies?"

"Me," Cole said softly. "I used to make cookies with my mom. I know how."

"Super. And you know what? She might have used the same family favorite recipe that she and I got from our mom. How about you, Molly? Want to help?"

"Not me." Molly headed for her room. "I'm going to read and pray that we get enough snow that school closes for the rest of the year."

Ethan turned up the heat of the windshield defroster and peered at the wall of white ahead of him. Following a snowplow had kept his speed at twenty-five, but the snow was too deep to try passing and he doubted he could make it through the drifts ahead of the plow anyhow. With such limited visibility he'd probably end up stuck in a ditch.

He'd passed the turnoff for Aspen Creek Park a few miles back, so the main highway would soon veer to the east, while Spruce Road continued north through the deepening forest for another mile to Hannah's place.

With only a couple homes on Spruce, it probably wasn't a high priority, and if the plow didn't head up that way, the rest of this trip was going to be a true test of what his rental SUV could do.

He'd probably end up finishing the trip on foot, or choosing the wiser course of giving up and turning back for town. How far would he get, trudging through this snow with a brace and a bum leg?

But if the forecasters were right and this storm worsened, how safe were Hannah and the kids up here in such an isolated area if the power went out, the furnace quit or her phone went dead?

If he didn't reach them now, he wouldn't rest easy back in town until he did.

Another blast of wind buffeted the side of his SUV and turned the visibility to zero. When the snow cleared he could see the plow rumbling away on the sharp curve to the east. Spruce Road opened up ahead of him like a white tunnel beneath an arched dome of the winter-bare branches of the trees lining either side.

He debated for a second then headed up the lane.

His prayers had never amounted to much—he doubted they'd even been heard much less answered. If God had listened, his best friends would still be alive.

But now he said one under his breath as he leaned forward to peer into the blinding world of white, his hands gripping the steering wheel.

The SUV steadily plowed through the snow, bucking through drifts, shimmying over ice patches. He passed a mailbox, then one more. The driveways leading back into the woods were obscured by drifts.

Finally he caught a faint view of a dead end sign through the falling snow and then Hannah's mailbox.

For the second time in years he said a prayer. And this time it was heartfelt thanks.

Gathering the grocery bags on the seat next to him,

Ethan stepped out into a knee-deep drift and his bad leg buckled. Only his grip on the SUV's door kept him upright.

He limped to the front entry, cringing at each step, and knocked. From inside came a cacophony of barking and the sounds of dogs clawing at the door. A moment later Hannah peeked through the small window.

She unlocked the door and stared at him in surprise. "What are you doing out in this weather? Have the plows come through already?"

"Just on the highway."

"And you still managed to make it up Spruce Road? That couldn't have been easy." With a twinkle in her eyes, she stepped aside to usher him in. "Especially for a Southern driver."

"It isn't that we can't drive in snow, we're just smart enough to live where it isn't an issue."

He set the groceries on the floor, shucked off his boots and hung his jacket on the coatrack by the door. He savored the aroma of warm chocolate chip cookies. "Who's baking?"

"Me and Aunt Hannah. Molly didn't want to help, so she went outside to see the chickens and the pony." Cole stared at Ethan from the kitchen then rushed to grab his own coat. "You got here! That means we can go sledding!"

"Not so fast, buddy." Ethan ruffled his blond hair. "I was really fortunate to get here. But the roads aren't good at all."

The boy's shoulders slumped. "We gotta have snow to go sledding. But then we *get* snow and we can't go anywhere. It isn't fair."

"There will be lots of other times. So many that you might even get tired of it, kiddo." Hannah nodded toward the window. "And, remember, your job is to watch out for the snowplow. Unless it comes too close to dark, we'll still try to go today."

Ethan hoped not. The thought of repeatedly trudging up a long hill only for a quick trip down made his knee throb as he carried the two grocery sacks to the kitchen counter. Though he forced himself to walk with a steady gait, he looked up and found Hannah's gaze riveted on his right leg. *Busted.*

"What happened to you? You weren't limping like that before."

"Took a wrong step when I got out of the SUV. It's nothing."

"Right. If you take a seat and prop up that leg on an ottoman, I'll give you a cold pack."

"It's fine."

"No, it's not. Sit." She fluffed up a couple of sofa pillows. "Chair or sofa?"

From her steely look of determination, he knew he might as well give in. "Chair, I guess. But no ice pack."

She put one pillow against the backrest, waited for him to get settled and then put the other pillow on the ottoman to elevate his leg.

She glanced at him. "Do you mind?"

He started to wave her away but she'd already crouched next to the ottoman. She studied his leg for a moment then ran deft hands down his jeans from mid-thigh to ankle, gently probing here and there.

Warmth radiated through him at her light, professional touch, and he found himself drawn to the way the flickering fire turned her hair to molten gold.

Then her light fingertips brushed over the mid-calf area of his right leg. He drew in a sharp breath and forced himself to not flinch.

Her gaze flew up to meet his. "Does it hurt here? Or…here?"

Always, but he wasn't about to admit it.

"So…what happened?"

He shrugged. "Shattered tibia and fibula. Took three surgeries to rebuild them."

"Would it be more comfortable if you took your brace off while you're resting?"

"No."

She gave a searching look. "So tell me about your pain meds."

"Huh?"

"Tell me about your pain meds," she repeated. "Do they give you adequate relief? Or have you been trying to taper?"

He set his jaw. "I quit the prescriptions right after I was discharged. I manage without anything, except for maybe an ibuprofen now and then."

"Toughing out pain isn't macho, Ethan. Not when something mild can help keep you moving so you can maintain your muscle mass, strength and mobility."

"Which I am doing."

She rose. "If you say so. But if you have problems, come to the Aspen Creek Clinic. Dr. Talbot is there Monday, Wednesday and Friday, and she's excellent. I'm usually there Monday through Friday."

Though he had no intention of going, he nodded. "I'll keep that in mind."

"And, of course, there's a VA hospital in the Twin Cities, plus some VA clinics that are a bit closer."

"Right."

She blew out a slow breath. "Why do I think it's a waste of time talking about this?"

"I've had good medical care, but I'm done. I figure that now it's up to me."

She frowned at him. "Let's move on to something easier then. Your jeans are damp from the snow—knees on down—so you must be chilled. Can I throw them in the dryer for you?"

"Uh...no. But thanks."

"I probably have a large enough robe around here someplace. Or maybe some sweatpants would be better." Her eyes twinkled and a flicker of a grin touched her lips. "I have hot pink or lime."

He snorted at that. "The jeans will dry."

"Not very fast, but suit yourself." She snagged a brightly colored lap quilt from the back of the sofa and draped it over his legs, threw another log on the fire and went into the kitchen. He could see her piling chocolate chip cookies on a plate.

"Coffee or cocoa?"

He shifted his attention to the crackling fire, thankful for the warmth radiating into the living room. "I'm good."

"No—make a choice. I've got cookies here, too."

"Coffee, I guess. Thanks. While you're over there, you might want to check those grocery sacks and put things away."

She lifted the edge of one of the sacks and peered inside. "Two dozen eggs, butter, a loaf of bread..."

"I wasn't sure if you were low on any of the basics, so I grabbed a few things in town in case you wouldn't be able to get out for a while."

"Thank you. This was so thoughtful." She cocked her head, listening to the wind howling outside, then prepared a hot cup of coffee for him with the Keurig machine on the counter. "And it was probably a really good idea. The wind wasn't supposed to pick up until later on, but it sounds like it's already here. I'm not sure if you'll even be able to make it back down the road to the highway, if you wait much longer. You should probably go right away."

"Not until I'm sure that you're all set for this weather. Do you have plenty of firewood?"

"There's a big stack in that alcove by the fireplace, and I've got two cords under a tarp next to the back porch." She gave him a plate with the mug of coffee and the cookies. "So we're good."

"What about all the animals? I can help you with chores before I go."

She smiled at that. "Thanks for the offer, but I think you'll want to keep off that leg for a while. There's not much to do—the chickens always roost inside the barn when it's this cold, so I just need to close the little door to their outside run. They already have free-choice feed and an electric waterer that doesn't freeze."

"What about the pony?"

"It's too early now, but before dark I'll close Penelope in for the night, bed her down and feed her. She can go in or out at will during the day, but the silly thing wants to stay outside no matter what—rain, sleet or snow. I just hate to think of her outside all night in the wind and cold."

Cole, still standing at the front windows, looked over his shoulder. "The plow still hasn't come. Why not?"

"They're probably taking care of all the main roads first, honey. Why don't you find a board game in your room or bring out your Legos? That would be a lot more fun than watching for the snowplow, wouldn't it?"

Cole's shoulders slumped as he disappeared into his room.

Ethan lifted his coffee in salute. "Perfect coffee. Cookies, too."

"Glad you like them." She glanced toward Cole's open bedroom door and then moved to the sofa next to Ethan's chair and leaned forward, her elbows braced on her thighs. She lowered her voice. "I was hoping I'd have a chance to talk to you privately. It's about Cole."

Ethan set his coffee cup on the small end table next to his chair. He already had a good idea about what she wanted to discuss, but he didn't have the answer. Not for sure. "The incident with the spilled cocoa last night?"

"Exactly. It broke my heart to see his reaction. He was so frightened—like he was expecting to be severely scolded. And it makes me worry about who—and when—someone treated him that way."

"I can't see my brother ever treating Cole like that. Distant? Yeah. Not giving the kid enough attention? Probably. Rob was usually caught up in his own big dreams and financial dramas."

"And Dee was a good mom, I'm sure of it. I visited whenever I could, and I never heard my sister raise her voice unless one of the kids was really out of line and refused to listen. They loved her to pieces. Cole followed her around like a little duckling."

"I saw that, too—what little time I was around."

Glancing at Cole's bedroom door again, where the sound of a battery-operated toy car now buzzed around the room, Hannah took a deep breath. "And that leaves your aunt Cynthia. And some babysitters, I suppose. But Dee didn't work outside the home, so there wouldn't have been many of those."

Ethan stared at the flames dancing in the fireplace, remembering Cynthia's anger when he and Rob had accidentally broken a vase while playing in her living room. He'd been in kindergarten, and facing her cold fury had made him feel like his world was about to end. "Cynthia means well. I can't imagine her laying a hand on anyone. But she's not Mary Poppins."

Hannah nodded. "I saw her at Rob and Dee's funeral, of course, and after that I went down several times over the summer to see Molly and Cole. As you can imagine, they were just devastated. But they were also shell-shocked and terribly withdrawn. I would have gone down to see them more often, but Cynthia privately told me—coldly *discouraged* me—from even that much contact. She said it only confused the children during such a fragile time. She said they were much worse after my visits."

"But she's not in the picture any longer. So what are you trying to say?"

"Just that Cole's fear over spilling the cup of cocoa worries me. A lot. And now you're here, talking about wanting to take the kids back to Texas. Where there are no grandparents to help you out. No other aunts or cousins or lifelong friends around, either."

"I can't instantly manufacture a support system, if that's what you're getting at."

"So where does that leave them, if you go back on active duty, or find a job, or simply want a date night with someone? I didn't ever see Cynthia screaming at the kids, but from the way she's treated me, I think it's a very distinct possibility that she might. If—by chance—you gain even partial custody, I want you to promise that woman will not have any lengthy contact with Molly and Cole."

"Agreed."

"And I…" Hannah faltered. "You do?"

She looked so surprised at his immediate acquiescence that he felt a sudden heaviness in his heart. Did she really think him so uncaring, so totally unsuitable to raise Molly and Cole?

"Whatever you think of me, I only want the best for them. And whatever her faults, I'm sure Cynthia wanted that, too. But she hasn't mellowed into a sweet, patient old lady, and I don't imagine she'd even want to have any part of caring for them in the future. So that case is closed. I promise."

"Still—" The sound of the little race car stopped and Hannah paused, listening.

"Hannah," Cole called out. "I need your help with Candy Land. It's up too high."

"Excuse me." Hannah rose and headed for Cole's room.

Curious about what she'd done for the boy's room with such short notice, Ethan swept aside the lap quilt and hobbled after her. He leaned a shoulder against the door frame and watched her reach for the game on a shelf, then he surveyed the room.

He felt his heart swell until it barely fit in his chest. It was everything he and Rob had never had as boys. Perfect for making Cole feel at home.

The walls were light blue, with a dinosaur wallpaper border along the top and dinosaur curtains on the double window facing the backyard.

The boyish furniture was rustic oak that could take a lot of abuse—a big dresser topped with a dinosaur-themed lamp and the kind of bunk bed with a place for a desk in its lower level. But instead of desk, a fort had been constructed in that space, complete with a window and camo-print canvas hanging across a little doorway.

Filling another wall, floor-to-ceiling shelves were

already filled with toys and books. It looked as if Cole had lived there all his life.

Hannah handed the board game to Cole. "Do you want to play in here or out by the fireplace?"

He promptly headed toward the living room. Hannah glanced at Ethan then studied the room. "Well, what do you think?"

"How did you ever get this ready so fast?"

"Craigslist and a lot of friends. This used to be my office, so it was loaded with my stuff, and the walls were pale peach with lacy curtains. As you can imagine, we worked like mad to make it into a boy's room."

The back door squealed open and slammed shut. Boots thumped onto the floor and then Molly came around the corner in stockinged feet, her cheeks rosy.

"You were out there a long time," Hannah said. "You must be really cold. Do you want some cocoa?"

"No thanks," Molly mumbled. She went into her room and shut the door behind her.

"Sorry about that. I would show you her room, but I guess we're still in an adjustment phase, so I'm going to just let her be for a while. With school on Monday on top of everything else, I think she needs some space."

In the living room Cole was setting up the game. He looked up at Hannah and Ethan with such hopefulness in his eyes that Ethan just couldn't say no.

Ethan smiled. "Can I play a round with you before I go?"

From outside at the front of the house came a loud *zzzzzt* and a bang. Instantly all of the lights went out and the refrigerator stopped humming. The lights flared on for a second then went dead.

Ethan jerked and spun around, adrenaline surging through him at the sound of enemy fire. The choking smell of smoke and blood, hot metal and burning rubber.

He was in the back of that doomed transport vehicle, trapped by the explosion and shrapnel—

"Are you okay?" Hannah murmured. Her hand hovered over his arm then she cautiously drew it back. "You know where you are, right?"

He blinked, confusion spinning through his brain. He forced himself to focus on her face and the turbulent emotions began to calm, leaving raw embarrassment in their wake.

The cats curled up in front of the fireplace had darted for hiding places. The two old dogs had barely stirred. And Cole was looking up at him as if he'd seen a ghost. "What was that sound outside?" he cried. "You were scared!"

"He was just surprised, Cole. That loud noise was probably because a tree limb fell over the power line close by." Hannah gave him a reassuring hug. "Or maybe it was a careless squirrel."

Cole's eyes widened. "A huge, monster squirrel? Like Godzilla?"

"Nope. Now and then a regular ole squirrel fries itself at the top of the tall power pole out in front—by touching the pole and the power line at the same time. It's happened three times in the past six months, so now maybe the power company will finally install the squirrel guard they've been promising."

She reached for her cell phone, scanned the directory and called the power company. After a five-minute wait she spoke to someone.

"Well, guys. They say there are lines down all over the county due to this storm, and thousands of people are without power. They won't get to us until sometime tomorrow, and that's if the road is plowed by then. Apparently the main roads in and out of town are drifted shut and the plows have stopped until the wind dies down."

Ethan stood at the front window and forced himself to concentrate on slow, steady breathing as he stared out at the heavy snowfall driven horizontal by the strong winds.

The curtain of snow obscured both his SUV and the county road that hit a dead end just past Hannah's house. And at just three o'clock, the daylight was already fading. "It's now or never, if I'm going to get back to town, but from the sound of things, it isn't worth trying."

Hannah joined him at the window. "Not if it's so bad the plows quit."

He frowned. "I'm glad to be here, though. I hate to think of you and the kids alone out here if anything goes wrong."

"We'll be fine—I've lived here for five years, and this storm isn't anything new, believe me. But I appreciate the concern." She went to the fireplace and added another log. "I'm going to let the pups run outside for a few minutes, then bring them in here to romp. Then I'll check the generator and get it ready, bring in more firewood and get the kerosene lamps set up. After that I'll go take care of the outside chores. I think you should either play Candy Land with Cole or go back to the chair and rest that leg."

"Candy Land it is." He laughed aloud. "But what a list you have. Reminds me of a country oldie I've heard on the radio about a guy giving his wife a long list of chores starting with 'Put another log on the fire...'"

She chuckled. "If memory serves, she's leaving him

by the end of that one. But my chores won't take too long."

She headed for the door leading to the garage and jerked to a halt. Then spun toward the window over the sink.

"Fire! Oh, no—*fire!*" Hannah jerked on her boots, hopping on one foot and then the other as she hurried to the back door. Shoving her arms into the sleeves of her jacket, she jerked up the zipper and wrenched open the door. "Call 9-1-1 and tell them the barn is on fire. Hurry. The fire number for this place is 478."

Ethan hurried after her, punching in 9-1-1 and making the call as he hobbled to his jacket and boots and pulled them on.

She was going into that blaze to save those stupid chickens and pony. She was as impetuous and foolhardy as she'd been thirteen years ago.

Only this time, it could kill her.

Chapter Seven

Hannah plowed through the wide, deep snowdrift in the backyard. It reached her upper thighs and each step was a struggle—as if she were trying to swim through a vat of thick, cold molasses. High winds threatened to knock her off her feet.

Ahead, the blaze licked at the walls of the barn on the two sides she could see. Something exploded inside—maybe an aerosol can, fueling the flames even higher.

Her heart clenched. She wasn't going to reach the animals in time. *Please, Lord, make Penelope go outside. And please help me save those poor chickens.*

She spared a quick glance over her shoulder. Ethan was closing the distance between them, his face grim. Back at the house, Molly and Cole stood in the open doorway to the deck, their faces pale with fear.

"If the dispatcher calls back with any questions, tell them the barn is on fire at Hannah Dorchester's place, Spruce Road," Ethan shouted back at them. "Got it? Dorchester. Fire number 478. Write it down—478. And shut that door!"

The wind slammed snow into Hannah's face and down her neck as she pivoted and again struggled toward the barn through the snow. Her lungs burning and throat raw with exertion in the cold, she'd begun to feel the searing heat of the blaze when Ethan closed a strong hand on her shoulder and pulled her to a halt.

"No," he shouted above the keening wind. "Don't!"

"I'm not stupid—I'm not going inside. If the hens are in their run, I've got to try to grab them and get them away from the heat. And I'm praying Penelope hasn't panicked and gone back into the barn. Do you see her?"

He scanned the area near the barn, squinting against the driving snow. "No—wait. Is that her back in the trees?"

Thickly covered in snow from ears to tail, Penelope looked more like the mound of a ski run mogul than a pony, but she'd stayed at the far end of her corral instead of running into the familiar safety of the barn. If it were true that some horses did that, at least Penelope had more common sense.

Hannah reached under her jacket and unbuckled her leather belt. "Can you reach her and put this around her neck? I'll come back for her in a minute. She's going to the garage."

"Wait!"

She ignored him and darted to the chicken run at the other end of the little barn, knowing there was little hope. The roosting chickens had probably already died from the smoke.

But now she heard angry squawking and the beating of wings against the chain-link fencing that formed a roof over the pen, meant to protect them from hawks and owls.

Wind-driven flames were already starting to reach this end of the barn and from somewhere inside she heard the screech of weakened timber giving way.

There's so little time. She slipped inside the outside pen through its narrow walk door. Grabbing two of the hens, she slowly made her way to a large, empty kennel inside the garage, fighting the deep snow and the wind that threatened to send her back two steps for each one forward. She locked them in a Great Dane–sized kennel and then hurried back for the final bird.

Ethan—now limping painfully as he made his way through the heavy snow—and Penelope arrived minutes later. Inside the garage Hannah sagged against the bumper of her SUV with exhaustion and relief.

"Penelope can wander around in here for the night, I guess. I've got a couple bales of cedar shavings I can put down in the corner on the far side for her, and some in the cage for the chickens. Not perfect, but it will do."

"Better here than out in a blizzard." Ethan scraped the thick blanket of snow off the pony's back and neck with the side of his hand. "That barn will be a total loss."

"I know." She looked into the high-walled pen where the pups were sleeping in a warm pile while their mother, Lucy, kept a watchful eye on Ethan and the pony. "At least everyone is safe. I'd better get inside and check on the kids. Molly ought to be old enough to keep an eye on Cole for a little while, but you never know."

The two were standing just inside the door when Hannah and Ethan walked in, their faces tense with worry.

"We were afraid you'd get burned up. The fireman called and said he couldn't come." Cole looked back and forth between Ethan and Hannah. "Is the pony okay? And the chickens, too?"

Hannah ruffled his blond hair. "They're fine. Now

they're up here in the garage where they can stay warm and dry tonight."

Cole's anxiety seemed to ease, but she wasn't sure about Molly.

Hannah gave her a closer look. It wasn't tension or fear on her face. It was misery. Sheer misery, coupled with overwhelming guilt. "Molly?"

"I didn't mean to do it. *Honest*." The girl's lower lip trembled and tears filled her eyes.

"You mean the fire?" Hannah exchanged glances with Ethan, then led Molly to a chair at the kitchen table and sat next to her while Cole and Ethan headed for the living room. "It could have started for a lot of different reasons. What could you have done to cause a fire?"

Molly's tears spilled down her face. "I thought the hens were too cold. Ruth kept fluffing up her feathers like she needed to be warmer and that funny-looking heater wasn't even very hot…but I couldn't find a way to turn it up. So I moved it closer to where they roost. What if it made their feathers catch fire?"

"I didn't see a single singed feather. They even had enough sense to flee to their outside pen."

"But—"

"A heat lamp with a bare bulb and no wire guard would be a big risk for sure. But the people who brought those hens here also brought the flat-panel heater from their coop, which is much safer. It's just mild, radiant heat that brings up the temp a few degrees."

"I…I thought…"

"Anything electrical could probably short out somehow, but if that happened to the heater, it wouldn't be your fault. Maybe there was some mouse damage to the wiring somewhere in the barn." Hannah rested a gentle hand on Molly's cheek. "I'll call the insurance company and fire department Monday morning. I'm sure they'll want to figure it out for the insurance claim. No worries, okay?"

"Where will the animals stay now? Will they be all right?"

"They'll be fine. After I get the snow cleared off the driveway tomorrow, I'll start parking outside, until I can figure out a replacement for the barn. That probably can't happen until spring, but we'll get by."

Molly nodded somberly.

"With all this excitement I haven't noticed the time. What would you like me to start for supper?"

"I'm not really hungry. But thanks, anyway."

Hannah sighed as she watched Molly go back to her room, then she rose and went to check on Cole. He and Ethan were on the floor, bathed in the warm light of the fireplace and well into a round of Candy Land. As always, Maisie was pressed close to Cole's side as if she knew how much hurt he still held inside.

The picture of Ethan and Cole, with their heads nearly together as they concentrated on the board game, made Hannah's heart squeeze.

She'd thought of Ethan as her nemesis for thirteen long years. Remembered every last detail of the weekend of his betrayal and his callous departure for active duty without a farewell, much less an apology.

He'd torn her heart in two.

Ever since she'd thought of him as heartless. Cruel. Someone she never wanted to see again. Someone she could never forgive.

Eventually she had, after a lot of prayer. But it had been a grudging forgiveness. An obligation, once she'd really thought about the words of the Lord's Prayer she said every night.

And then Ethan showed up on her doorstep two days ago and turned her safe world upside down.

Her heart had warned her to stay clear of him from that very first moment. Yet…he was a warrior, one who had sacrificed for his country. One who—like all soldiers—deserved the heartfelt thanks of every American, including her. Even if she wished he'd leave Aspen Creek and never come back.

But now she'd seen another side of him and wondered if she'd been wrong about him all along.

A cruel man didn't play Candy Land with a little boy and clearly try to lose.

A heartless man didn't trudge through deep snow, feeling pain with every step, to rescue an elderly pony, or try to break through a young girl's shell of grief and loss with gentle words.

Her cell phone chimed, pulling her out of her troubled thoughts.

"Bill Jacobs here. Fire department." She'd known the fire chief and his wife Marnie since her EMT days, before she'd gone on to her hectic clinical phase of study at Mayo.

She smiled into the phone. "I'll bet you're having a busy day."

"Too much. Family of five—their dog woke them up late this morning before they all died of carbon monoxide poisoning. I'm still thanking God for that dog. Three little kids, right before Christmas…" He swallowed hard. "Then there was a fire at the apartments west of town and we had to call for trucks from two other towns for that one. And then Keeley North's dad wandered off this afternoon. In the middle of a blizzard, no less."

Hannah drew in a sharp breath. "Please tell me he's all right."

"Dr. Talbot was covering the ER when we finally found him and brought him in. Frostbite, hypothermia, but he'll be okay. She said he's too cantankerous to die."

"Poor Keeley. She must have been beside herself."

"While I was still there, she was talking to the doc about finding a memory care unit for him." Bill sneezed. "Anyway, I'm real sorry we couldn't make it out on your call—we were already spread too thin and the snow is so bad I don't think we could've even made it up your road. If it had been a house fire, we would have tried hard to get there. But I understand it was that old shed out back?"

"Small barn. We didn't lose any animals, but I'm sure it's a total loss. I'll call the insurance company tomorrow."

"Is it still actively burning anywhere?"

"Once the roof and framework were gone, I could see the hay smoldering. After all the wet snow falling on the hay, I imagine it will continue for some time. There's nothing else close to the barn at risk, though."

"I'll try to get out there tomorrow, too, in case there's any question about how it started. Will you be at the clinic or at home?"

"Clinic. But I'm just working nine to three Monday through Friday until New Year's because my niece and nephew are here. Permanently, I hope."

"The wife and I were real sorry to hear the news about your sister." He hesitated, cleared his throat. "Just a warning—you know that Gladys Rexworth will surely hear about your fire from some gossip or another. She'll think it's a good excuse to stir up the city council again about shutting down your rescue operation."

"She's already tried, but I'm licensed and have passed every inspection, and so have the other two women who take in strays. She and the rest of the city council should just be thankful they don't have to add a shelter to their annual budget. Though, if the town grows any more, they'll need to."

"And cut back on their beautification projects? They'd consider that a bitter pill." He snorted. "But I've got to say one thing—Gladys seems to have a very personal vendetta against you, and I'd hate to be in your shoes. Any idea what got her started?"

"Um...can't say," she told him.

Which was completely true, and long after the call ended, Hannah stared out the window at the deepening dusk.

She knew full well why Gladys had held on to her grudge. Why she had tried to ruin Hannah's career at the clinic with her gossip, and would now try again to end the animal rescue out of sheer spite.

But because of strict medical privacy laws, there wasn't a thing Hannah could do to stop her.

Ethan helped Hannah set up the generator outside, in the lee of the garage, to maintain the electricity for the appliances, water heater and well pump, since the power was still out.

The fireplace, Hannah said, was usually adequate for enough warmth so the water pipes didn't freeze, though everyone would be wearing warm sweaters and extra socks.

While she let the dogs and puppies outside for a brief run and filled their food and water dishes, he brought several armloads of firewood inside and filled the two kerosene lanterns.

Now the pups were running helter-skelter through the house, sliding on the hardwood floors and yipping at each other as they wrestled. Cole was in the midst of the melee, nearly bowled over by their sloppy puppy kisses and trying to hold a pudgy little brown-and-white one that was wriggling in his arms.

The cats had immediately disappeared in the face of the onslaught pouring in the door. The basset hound hadn't stirred from his warm spot by the fireplace.

Old Maisie had retreated to the fireplace as well, clearly overwhelmed by all the exuberance.

"I'm going to start supper," Hannah announced, peering into the refrigerator. "We've still got lots of leftovers to use up from dinner on Friday, if that's all right with everyone. After that, we've got several pans of lasagna and some casseroles that friends dropped by for the freezer. Let's eat in about an hour, okay?"

"All sounds good to me." Ethan surveyed the flashlights and candles sitting on the kitchen counter, then shouldered on his coat. "It looks like you're all set in here, but I'd like to check out your garage and see if something better could be done for the pony. I noticed the plywood walls of the puppy pen. Is there any extra plywood out there? Or extra 2x4s?"

"Stacked against the south wall and also up in the eaves. I can come out to help as soon as I get this all started."

"Can I help?"

Cole looked up him with such longing that Ethan felt his heart catch. Was the boy missing the days of projects with his dad, or was it that he longed for the male companionship that Rob had rarely shared? "Of course, buddy. I need a helper and you'll be perfect. Put your jacket and boots on, though."

Out in the garage Ethan discovered Penelope in the narrow space between Hannah's SUV and the house, with her head deep into one of the garbage cans, its aluminum lid on the floor and much of the contents scattered at her feet.

"Looks like you're having a good time," he muttered, tossing the trash back into the can and settling the lid on tight. "If this means you'll be having a bellyache, I don't think your vet will be making house calls tonight."

Across the garage he discovered the stack of 2x4s and a couple sheets of plywood. Eyeballing the back corner of the garage, he cut some of the wood with a handsaw then began building an L-shaped framework that could support sections of plywood four feet tall and eight feet long.

Cole appeared at his elbow. "Can I hammer something?"

"You bet. Watch out for your fingers, though." Ethan steadied the boards while Cole gave a nail a tentative tap then missed the nail entirely. "Good job. This is really hard with such a heavy hammer and that little nail. Try again."

Cole sent a worried look at Ethan and then whacked at the nail again, sending it sideways.

"I guess I don't know how."

"Everyone starts out like this—and with practice, learns to do better. Your dad and I didn't do half as good as you when we were your age."

"Really?"

"Really. It just takes time. And maybe a smaller hammer." Ethan searched the small workbench near the puppy pen and found a lighter tack hammer. "Try this one."

Cole two-handed it and missed the nail then hit it on the second try with a resounding thwack.

"That, my man, was excellent."

Beaming, Cole tried it several more times before putting down the hammer. "My arms are tired," he confessed. "Sorry."

"I could still use your help, though. The nails are in that red bucket by your feet. Can you hand them to me, one by one? This will go a lot faster and then Penelope can have her own stall tonight."

Cole nodded, his face filled with pride.

The pony wandered over and stood behind Ethan to oversee the project, her warm breath and muzzle whiskers tickling the back of his neck. In an hour the simple framework was assembled, the plywood panels hammered onto the frame.

The door into the house opened and Hannah stepped out into the garage. "Wow. That is amazing, you two. It's perfect!"

Cole looked up at her with shy pride. "I'm just the helper."

"And he's really good at it, too. Without Cole I couldn't have done half as much." He gestured to a three-foot opening on one side. "This is for a gate, but I couldn't find any spare hinges on the workbench."

"I don't think there are any. Did you look in the buckets of odds and ends under the workbench?"

"No luck. I figured I could temporarily suspend the door—" he held up a section of plywood "—and fasten it on both sides with hook-and-eye closures, like the ones for old-fashioned screen doors. I found a few of those. The next time you go to town, you could pick up a couple of proper hinges."

"Thank you, thank you," she said fervently. "I really

didn't like the thought of the pony roaming the garage all night. The cement floor is just too hard for her old bones and she could get into all sorts of trouble."

Hannah picked a heavy, plastic-wrapped bale of compressed pine-shaving bedding from a stack at the front of her SUV, slit it open in the new stall, then got two more bags while Ethan finished the temporary gate.

After fluffing the bedding with a pitchfork, the hard bale of shavings expanded into a deep, soft bed so the pony could comfortably lay down. Hannah put her hands on her hips and surveyed the results. "This is fantastic, Ethan and Cole. I'm so grateful to you both. Especially as it could be months before it's warm enough to start building a new shed."

Cole grinned from ear to ear at her praise. "Can she have some of the hay by the puppy pen?"

"Since all the rest of the hay in the barn is probably smoldering, yes, indeed. I'm so glad I brought up so many bales to insulate the outside walls of that pen."

Ethan glanced around for a bucket. "Can I use that for the pony's water?"

Hannah nodded. "I'll get it—I'll need to fill it from the bathtub faucet, and it will be heavy."

He raised an eyebrow.

"Look, you might be a tough guy, but I see you limping worse than ever. As much as I appreciate your help, going out to the barn through those drifts didn't do that leg any favors."

She grabbed the bucket before he could get to it and grinned. "It's time to come in for supper, anyway, and probably time for that ice pack you didn't want."

Chapter Eight

"I don't know how many times Molly asked about school tomorrow," Hannah murmured as she snuggled deeper under her afghan on the sofa and sipped a cup of hot cocoa. "I wonder if she'll even sleep tonight."

"At least there should be a two-hour delay or a cancellation," Ethan said.

"Just more hours for her to worry about her entrance into enemy territory." Remembering the words of the older girl on the carriage ride, Hannah had offered to call some church friends and track down Joanie, who was apparently Molly's age. Would Molly want to think up some random questions about school to ask her, as a way to make contact?

Mortified, Molly had violently shook her head at that, saying Joanie would think her a total loser if she needed her aunt to find her a friend. Then she'd announced she was going to bed.

"I've already been told that I can drop her off in front of the school, but I was *not* to go in and embarrass her." Hannah sighed. "The elementary school actually wants parents to bring children inside and make sure their names are checked off, and the same routine after school. But Molly wants me to be invisible. Was I ever like that when I was her age? I hope not."

"Ask your mom." A corner of Ethan's mouth lifted in a quick grin. "You might be surprised."

"Actually, I wouldn't be, now that I think about it. Dad tolerated no back talk, no straying from proper behavior and absolutely no shirking of duties. I was more like a cadet than a daughter whenever he was around."

"How did your mom feel about that?"

"I'm sure my parents loved each other in their own way, but Mom is like a different person now that he's gone."

"Losing him must have been tough on her."

"Yeah, of course. But now it's like she's blossomed. She earned a Master's degree in nursing and moved to Minneapolis. Every time I talk to her on the phone she's happily volunteering for something, or going off to some social event. I guess she must have felt like she was under Dad's thumb, too."

Ethan looked at her and their eyes met, held. "So you were being honest when you said the reprieve from eloping with me really was all for the good. Right?"

Her pulse stumbled. "Honestly? It broke my heart. Maybe things would have been different for us. Better. I was sure of it at the time. But afterward I focused on my regimented childhood and figured I'd just been blessed with a fortunate escape."

His mouth quirked. "Ouch."

The wind continued to howl outside, buffeting the house with snow. The intimacy of this night, with the house darkened except for the soft glow of the kerosene lantern on the kitchen counter and the flickering fireplace, made it easier to talk about wounds that had never quite healed.

"Why did you do it? I used to wonder, a lot. Was I such a terrible mistake? Had you already started seeing the woman you married?"

"I was stupid. Too young. You were everything I'd ever wanted—more than I ever could have hoped for. But I knew nothing about marriage. Nothing about lifetime commitment. I sure didn't have an example of that at home, and I was terrified of being a failure." He stared into the fire. "Of failing you."

"So you ran."

"That afternoon I heard I had to report for duty by five—a week sooner than expected. So, yes, I ran. Didn't know how to explain or apologize. I knew I could face an enemy in combat but had no idea how to face you."

"So I was that fierce," she teased gently.

"You were that sweet and beautiful. And trusting. I threw away something I knew I'd never find again."

Her chest tightened and her throat felt too thick with emotion to speak.

He shook his head slowly. "So now—"

From Cole's bedroom came a terrified scream. And then another, even louder. Maisie hurried out of his room to Hannah's side and pawed at her, clearly indicating her worry.

Ethan blanched, his gaze darting around the room.

Hannah raced from the couch into Cole's room with Ethan and the dog at her heels.

His wide eyes glazed and unseeing, Cole was sitting up in his bunk bed with the blankets twisted around him. Flailing his arms, he seemed to be trying to fend off a legion of unseen monsters, his screams going on and on in the darkness.

Hannah moved next to him. "Everything is all

right," she murmured in a low voice. "You're at your aunt Hannah's house, in a nice, warm bed. Your uncle Ethan is here, too, so you are very safe."

But the inconsolable screaming didn't stop. If anything, his screams escalated.

"He probably doesn't really hear me, but I just want to offer comfort," Hannah said as she glanced at Ethan over her shoulder.

"Poor kid. Is he sick? In pain? Do we need to get him to the ER?"

"Night terrors," she said quietly, though Ethan could probably barely hear her. "First time since he got here, but don't worry—they aren't uncommon."

Ethan moved to her side. "Like a nightmare?"

"Not really. He's not awake, and he won't remember this in the morning." She gently circled one of his trembling wrists with her hand. "Poor guy. His pulse is racing."

"Shouldn't you wake him up?"

"I know it's hard to listen to him screaming, but he'll settle down eventually and still be asleep. If I try to force him awake, he might be confused and scared, and unable to get back to sleep for a long while. So if this ever happens when I'm not around, don't talk loudly or try to shake him awake. And if he gets out of bed, just quietly guide him back."

Ethan's eyes filled with helplessness and worry. "How do you...?"

"I've had a number of parents come into the clinic with kids who do this. It's sometimes just random. Sometimes it's from stress or fear, or sleeping in a strange place. Or big life changes."

"And Cole has faced all of that, and more," Ethan said somberly.

"For all I know, he might have had night terrors many other times, even before his parents passed away, though my sister never mentioned it." She looked at Cole, whose screams were quieting. "I think this bunk bed was a mistake if he is going to be experiencing these now and then. Some kids and adults will fall out of bed or even sleepwalk. He's too high up for that."

Cole still stared sightlessly ahead, but then he hiccupped and finally lay back down.

"This is going to be tricky, Ethan. But let's let him be quiet and settle down for a few minutes, then I wonder if you can reach up there and quietly pick him up while I pull his mattress down to the floor. Tomorrow I'll turn that lower bunk level into a regular bed."

"I wish he wouldn't scream like that," Molly mumbled from the doorway. "He wakes me up and then gives *me* nightmares just listening to him."

Hannah gently rubbed Cole's back. "I'm sorry, honey, but I think it's all over now. Go back to bed, okay?"

She yawned and gave Cole a bleary look. "Cynthia took him to the doctor right away when he did this. But there wasn't anything wrong."

"Did he ever have these problems before your parents' accident?"

"I dunno. I never heard him." Molly shrugged and shuffled back to her room.

It was nearly midnight by the time Cole was settled in his bed on the floor, with an arm flung over Maisie, who had curled up next to him. Her lips whiffled softly with doggy snores.

"That was quite an experience," Ethan said on a long sigh as they left Cole's room.

"And after quite a day. Are you sure you'll be okay on the sofa? There's a little room upstairs with a single bed if you'd rather, but that room is mostly storage. It'll be really cold."

He laughed at that. "Believe me, the sofa and that big stack of blankets on it or that upstairs room would be ten times better than any place I had to sleep in Iraq."

"Can I get you any acetaminophen or ibuprofen?"

"I'm good."

She lingered just inside the living room. "Um, if you get hungry, help yourself to anything in the cupboards or fridge. Especially the turkey. I don't think we'll ever be able to finish all of it."

Cole's night terror episode had been a perfect lead-in to the questions she wanted to ask, but now it was late and she could only imagine how uncomfortable it was for Ethan to be still standing on that bad leg, no matter what he claimed.

"Good night, Ethan. If you need more blankets or different pillows, you'll find them in the hall closet."

He crossed his arms and gave her an assessing look. "Well, what is it?"

"What?"

"You look like you've wanted to say something for the past half hour. You might as well get it over with." He lifted an eyebrow. "If you'd rather I didn't stay, I can start up your snowblower and work on the drive, and then see what that SUV can do about getting me back to town."

"No way. The last time I looked, some of the drifts were well over three feet, and it must be worse close to town. The fire chief told me hours ago that the main highway to town was already impassable. Anyway, the kids are happy that you're staying for the night."

"Then, what is it?"

She edged into the living room, sat on the arm of

one of the chairs and squared her shoulders. "I know it isn't my place to pry. But I couldn't help but notice your reactions the moment the power went out with a bang. Or when Cole started screaming."

He took the other chair, his eyes never leaving her face. "And?"

"Both times, it seemed like you'd been transported back to a different place. Like you weren't even here."

"Is that a problem for you?" he asked.

She raised a hand in frustration. "You're being obtuse. You have to know what I'm getting at."

He didn't answer.

"You were in a dangerous part of the world. You were badly injured," she continued doggedly. "You must have seen and done things the rest of us can't even imagine. So I'd guess PTSD is a part of your life now. And after an explosion close enough to take your hand, a traumatic brain injury—concussion—would not be unexpected. So is a TBI in your picture, too?"

"You were right in the first place. It isn't really your place to pry."

She huffed out an impatient breath. "Well, then. Let me try again. You were at Walter Reed for how many months? Before Rob and Dee's car accident, and you said you were released sometime this month. So...seven months, maybe eight?"

He looked away.

"I don't think anyone could have gone through all you did without some PTSD and a concussion—possibly severe—from such a close-proximity blast. They must have assessed you carefully and provided treatment. Did they say anything about long-term effects? Did they send you to support groups? A counselor?"

When he didn't reply, she had her answer. "Of course

they did, but you either didn't attend or didn't participate when you did go."

A muscle ticked along the side of his jaw.

"I'm not trying to badger you or sound like an interfering mother, honest." She gave a self-deprecating laugh. "I just want to know where you're at with this, because you want time with the kids. You even say you want full custody, though I plan to oppose that every step of the way because I feel they'll be happier here in the country. Near a close-knit, friendly little town instead of some big-city condo. But during whatever amount of time they spend with you, are you truly capable of keeping them safe?"

"Of course I am," he said, his voice level.

"I know you mean that, and you want it to be true. But I also know that blast injuries can cause a big list of long-term repercussions with TBI, and that PTSD can last for decades, especially if not addressed. Depression, episodes of irritability, anger issues and memory loss are just a few…and they can make family life difficult. So again, I'm asking. How are you, really? I want to know if you really are capable of dealing with these kids, or if your goal of custody is based on a sense of duty and responsibility to your brother."

He scrubbed a palm down his face then leaned forward and propped his elbows on his thighs. "Yes, I had a concussion—they tell me I was knocked out for about an hour. But after that I was in a hospital for a long time—plenty of time for that to heal. All of my symptoms—the headaches, dizziness, vertigo, confusion—were gone in a couple weeks."

"Thank goodness," Hannah breathed. "I'm glad to hear it."

"As for the PTSD, how common is that these days?

I'm working past it month by month. It doesn't affect me every day. And I'm not the only soldier who hasn't wanted the support groups—I've heard only fifty percent of us actually seek help."

"The effect can last for decades, Ethan. Some people never realize how much better they could feel if they only sought help."

He shrugged. "Maybe I am startled by loud noises. It's self-preservation for anyone after being in the Middle East so long. And who wouldn't have nightmares after some of the things you see over there? But I've been dealing with it on my own and doing fine. End of story."

"I see."

"So you don't need to worry about it. I promise you I have no issues that affect my ability to take care of the kids. None." He glanced at his wristwatch. "And with that, I'd like to turn in. It's been a long day."

"Good night." She hesitated, wanting this conversation to end on a more casual note, but then headed for her room. She shut the door quietly and leaned on it, thinking over all he'd done and said since first arriving at her door.

Funny, how people changed. He'd been a handsome daredevil when they'd first met—the kind of bad boy who could light up a movie screen or make a girl fall in love and want to take off on wild and crazy adventures with him, whatever the danger.

But he was different now. A man seasoned by years in the military, a man driven by responsibility and honor to right the wrongs of his irresponsible brother.

And he was a man with a good heart, who could be kind and gentle with kids and animals, yet still possessed the kind of indefinable charisma that drew her as much now as it had thirteen years ago. Even more so, as a man instead of the reckless boy he'd once been.

But between the two of them, he was *not* the one who should have custody of the children.

So whatever her personal attraction to him, she couldn't lose sight of her most important goal: helping Molly and Cole adapt to their new life in Aspen Creek. And making sure they felt loved and secure, before a caseworker arrived to judge whether or not this move had been the right one.

And she had just thirty days to do it.

Ethan stared at the flickering light of the fireplace long after Hannah said good-night, an ugly torrent of dark memories and troubled emotions making it impossible to sleep. He'd managed to bury all of it in some deep recess of his mind, where it could no longer take over his every waking thought and visit him in nightmares.

But now Hannah's persistent questions had set it all free.

Or maybe it had happened because he'd seen the terror on Cole's face and had heard him screaming inconsolably on and on and on, until he'd finally fallen back onto his pillow, exhausted. What kind of childish horrors had spun through his brain to incite such fear?

Ethan knew all too well about nightmares and the true horrors of this world.

Wounded and dying women and children, the heartbreaking collateral damage of war. Body parts and rivers of blood, and young men barely old enough to vote screaming in pain, begging for help as they lay dying. Begging for the chance to go home again.

His two best buddies—who had died because of him.

He'd seen the insurgent lob a grenade into the back of the transport vehicle. He'd lunged for it. But the others crammed inside had been dozing and he hadn't been able to crawl over them in time to throw it out.

The explosion had turned that vehicle into a scene of carnage.

If he'd only moved faster, he could have prevented it. If he could have fought off his loss of consciousness, he could have stemmed arterial wounds and saved the lives of his two closest buddies.

But he'd failed, and the crushing guilt would be like an anvil in his chest forever.

Chapter Nine

A̲t seven the next morning Hannah started a pot of coffee and checked the local weather—clear and cold—and the closing announcements on the laptop she kept on the kitchen counter.

With the schools still planning a two-hour delay, she could let the kids sleep in a while longer, though if the county plow didn't come by they wouldn't need to worry about going anywhere at all.

Ethan was already outside using the snowblower, though from the looks of things it was barely making a dent in the deep snowdrift that had crossed the front yard and banked halfway up the windows along the side of his SUV.

After calling the clinic to let the receptionist know she wouldn't be in until ten at the earliest, she began her morning routine of letting the dogs and puppies outside, cleaning cages and litter boxes, and filling the food and water dishes.

Penelope nickered when Hannah appeared in the garage, anticipating her special, geriatric horse pellets, which were now likely a pile of ash. Hannah brought her more hay, water and a handful of baby carrots as a treat.

"Sorry," she murmured as she rubbed just the right spot behind the pony's furry ears. "No pellets today."

The pony suddenly swiveled her ears and snorted, her head high. And soon Hannah could hear it, too—the distant, familiar rumble of a snowplow making its way up Spruce Road.

"Well, old girl—looks like you're in luck. We'll be able to get into town and get you more feed, after all."

At ten fifteen Hannah stamped the snow from her boots in the entryway of the Aspen Creek Clinic and then stopped at the front desk for a printout of her patient schedule.

The waiting room walls were now strung with clear Christmas lights and jewel-toned metallic ornaments hung from the ceiling over the reception counter and the office area behind it.

Hannah admired the sparkly lights. "Wow—great job of decorating, Connie."

"I'm only halfway done. Wait till you see this place tomorrow."

"I can't wait. Sorry about the delay getting here. Did you have to reschedule many of my patients?"

"Most of them were country people who were snowed in and couldn't make it into town, either." The fifty-something receptionist glanced at her computer screen. "And those who live in town sounded just as happy not to brave the roads. I cleared the schedule until eleven just in case you were delayed even further, so now you've got some time to catch your breath. How did it go with the kiddos this morning?"

"You raised three kids. How in the world did you manage?" Hannah rolled her eyes. "I felt like a field commander. Getting them fed, dressed and loaded into the car was quite a feat, because neither of them wanted to go to school."

"Your niece is in sixth grade, right? Tough age for a new school—especially midyear."

"I know. She was so nervous about walking into school—but adamant about me not going in with her. I'm praying that she'll find some friendly faces in her classes."

Connie offered a sympathetic smile. "Middle school years are the worst. And Cole?"

"First grade. Parents and guardians need to walk in with the younger kids, so I'm glad about that. I got to introduce him to his new teacher, and I saw a few boys I know from church, so I introduced him to them, too."

Connie tapped the tip of a pencil against her lips. "You know, I think my neighbor has a first-grader. Maybe we can get them together for a playdate sometime."

"That would be wonderful." Hannah glanced at her watch. "I need to make a few phone calls, so I'll be in my office."

"Oh…and, Hannah?" Connie's voice wafted down the hall. "So sorry to hear about your fire. I heard about it on the scanner."

Hannah walked past the first four exam rooms to her office and stepped inside, feeling, as always, a little rush of pleasure at having this private space to call her own. At her first job, in the next town over, she'd shared a cramped office with the director of nursing. No windows, no extra space, and the dreary mustard walls had made each day depressing. But here she'd been allowed to decorate just as she wished.

The walls were now a bright ivory that made the most of the sunshine streaming through the two large windows facing the west. She'd found the L-shaped oak desk and matching wall of bookshelves at an estate sale.

She sank into the leather swivel chair behind her desk and flipped through the pile of message slips, copies of new doctor's orders, today's hospital admission list and assorted mail left in a pile on her desk, then listened to her phone messages.

It looked like a busy day, so far.

Eight scheduled clinic appointments, afternoon rounds in the small, ten-bed hospital wing, with four patients to see there, and two quarterly assessments for residents in the twenty-bed, long-term-care unit.

At the sound of footsteps coming down the hall, she looked up and smiled. "Connie, could you check with—"

But it wasn't Connie who stood glowering at her from the open doorway.

"Gladys." Hannah cleared her throat. "Is there something I can do for you?"

"Certainly not." The woman breezed into the office and planted her hands on the back of one of the barrel chairs, her long, red-lacquered nail digging deep into the upholstery. "I'm no longer a patient at this clinic, to my relief."

In her seventies, with the austere, patrician elegance of someone wealthy and powerful, Gladys never hesitated to make a scene, and never seemed to care who saw it.

At least there weren't any patients waiting in the nearby exam rooms.

Hannah waited as the woman glanced around the office and sniffed her displeasure.

"I just wanted you to know that I've heard about your

little debacle yesterday, and how you've risked the lives of those poor animals in your care."

"Debacle?" Hannah blinked. "A shed on my property caught fire. No animals were even in it. Not one animal was harmed."

As usual, the woman ignored her. "I'm appalled at your so-called rescue operation. Amateurs have no business placing homeless animals at risk. I've called the state inspectors—again—and expect they will be visiting you very soon. You will see, missy, that you aren't so powerful as you think."

She was back to harping on their unfortunate, shared past history. *Again.*

Dr. Martin, long since retired, had apparently caved to her every whim regarding her prescriptions—probably to ensure her hefty donations to the hospital continued. The hospital had profited well—case in point, the new hospital wing named in her family's honor.

But Dr. Martin hadn't done her any favors.

Powerful sleeping pills, antianxiety meds, pain meds—she'd been insistent on them all, and livid when Hannah had refused to provide refill prescriptions. That Hannah had alerted Dr. Martin's replacements about the situation had been the last straw as far as Gladys was concerned.

When Gladys could no longer use her wealth to get whatever she wanted, she'd started going somewhere else for her health care. Hannah prayed it was someplace good.

"If you did call the state, that's fine." Hannah sighed. "As you know already, I have my nonprofit animal shelter license, as do the other two women in town who volunteer to help with rescues. We've each been properly inspected and approved, after meeting the required standards of care. We pay our annual fees."

Gladys drew herself up, reminding Hannah of a huffy bantam hen. "We shall see about that. I know that—"

Connie appeared in the doorway, tentatively waving a slip of paper. "Excuse me—so sorry to interrupt. I have an emergency message from the doctor. Can you pick up line three? It's urgent. And private."

Gladys glowered at Hannah, then pivoted and strode out of the office, her high heels clicking down the hallway.

"Is that really a message?" Hannah asked dryly.

Connie swept imaginary perspiration from her forehead. "No. But I could hear that woman clear down at the reception desk and figured you'd want her gone before patients started arriving. What's with her, anyway? Just because she's on the city council doesn't mean she can run roughshod over people."

"She's unhappy about a lot of things, I guess—but not about anything I can change. I just keep praying that she will mellow...or finally see the errors of her ways. But I'm beginning to doubt it will ever happen."

By three o'clock Hannah was finished for the day and more than eager to pick up Cole and Molly at school.

She'd worried about them all day, hoping they liked their teachers and had found it easy to find some new friends and gain acceptance, so important at their ages.

She'd just said farewell to Connie and started out the door when she heard the phone ring behind her and the loudspeakers crackle.

"Code Orange—ER. Code Blue—ER. Code Orange—ER."

A mass casualty, with at least one critical patient heading for the ER.

She turned around to find Connie gripping the phone receiver, her face white as chalk. "A van with a family of six kids. T-boned by a dually pickup at an icy intersection. One ambulance and three EMT units on the way. ETA fifteen minutes."

Hannah hesitated.

Ethan was the only other adult the kids had met in this town, besides their teachers or, briefly, Keeley and Sophie, who would still be at work.

He was only one they would recognize and trust to pick them up at school.

But the risk was clear.

Would he recall this day, and use it to prove to the caseworkers that Hannah's job made it too difficult for her to provide care for them in an emergency? Would he twist this to his benefit?

But there was no one else she could ask, and she'd have to deal with that later.

She whipped out her cell phone, checked the directory and scrawled a cell number for Connie. "Ethan Williams is the children's uncle from Dallas, and he's in town. Please call him. Ask him to pick up the kids at school, and give him the directions. Tell him I don't know when I'll be done here, but I'll try to text."

"But the schools—will they let a stranger do that?"

"Please call the school to explain. They'll see the hospital number on their caller ID. But text me if I need to call them personally."

And then Hannah began to run.

His mission had been a success, despite wary assessments by the principals at both schools and their demand that he show his driver's license.

Ethan looked at the two kids in his rearview mirror. "How was your first day at school?"

Total silence.

"Okay, what was the best part? There must have been something good."

Not one peep.

"Something bad?" It was probably wrong to ask, but now he was curious.

"I hated it," Molly ground out.

"Why?"

"It was just like when we moved back to Dallas last spring. Everyone looks at you like you're weird or have a disease. They whisper to each other about it and stare at you. And I just want to die." She shrugged. "You asked."

"That bad, huh."

She folded her arms over her chest. "I'm not going back there again. If you make me, I'm gonna run away, and then everyone will be sorry."

"I see." He kept a solemn face as he mulled over her words, sorry about her unhappiness but also amused at her childish logic. "So where would you go? It's mighty cold and snowy outside."

She glared at him.

"Well, then, how about you, Cole? What was the best part of today at school?"

"Chicken nuggets."

"Anything else?"

"We couldn't have recess outside, but we played dodgeball in the gym."

"Sounds like a good first day to me." He turned to look over his shoulder at the two of them. "Okay, then, now that you're buckled in, where would you like to go? Are you hungry?"

Molly dropped her chin down to the backpack she

held on her lap, face glum. Cole darted a glance at him then looked away.

"The thing is, I don't have a key to Hannah's house, though she might have one hidden somewhere outside. But she isn't answering her phone so I can't take you out there just yet."

The backseat remained silent.

"So what do you think of this? Hannah said the pony's feed was lost in the fire, and I don't think she's had time to buy more. So, we could go to the feed store outside of town and buy some sacks of whatever it is that Penelope eats. Then we could go to the malt shop and get whatever you want."

"Could we play a game there?" Cole's voice was barely audible, but the hope in his eyes touched Ethan's heart.

"Of course. And after that we could go back to that hardware store and see if we can find us all some ice skates. I saw the rink in the town square on my way to pick you two up, and it looked pretty nice. What do you say?"

Molly fidgeted. "I don't know how to skate."

"I don't, either," Cole piped up.

"Neither do I, but I'll bet we can learn."

"What if kids from school are skating?" Molly pleaded, clearly thinking it would be a social disaster. "They'll think I look really dumb."

After he finally coaxed an agreement from both of them, he drove to the feed store, where the clerk knew Hannah well and looked up her account to figure out which feed Ethan needed to buy.

At the malt shop, the kids each ordered hot-fudge sundaes with extra whipped cream, then only ate half before going back to play the pinball machines.

From the sounds of the chimes, they weren't scoring, but at least they seemed enthralled by the colorful lights.

Keeping one eye on the kids, Ethan opened the new paperback he'd bought today, but his thoughts kept straying to the call from the hospital receptionist.

A horrific accident.

Victims being stabilized, four leaving the local hospital by helicopter. Several surgeries being dealt with here…and Hannah was in the thick of it.

He hadn't realized what a range of services PAs could provide, much less that she was qualified to assist the doctor performing the emergency surgeries. But the receptionist had certainly filled him in, leaving him with the uncomfortable feeling that he'd been underestimating Hannah from the first time they'd met. Irresponsible? Flighty and immature?

Maybe back then, but she'd also been bright. She'd charted her course, buckled down and now carried a lot of responsibility on her delicate shoulders.

He could no longer discount her out of hand as someone who couldn't handle the responsibility of taking on Molly and Cole.

Not that he planned to give up.

A group of kids came into the malt shop, laughing and jostling each other as they headed for the pinball machines. Molly and Cole promptly returned to Ethan's side.

"You don't want to play anymore? I could go over there with you, if you want."

"No." Molly shook her head. "Can we leave? *Please?"*

"Okay. Next up, skates at the hardware store."

Which turned out to be more complicated than he'd thought, and a lot more expensive.

Still, the young clerk seemed knowledgeable and

took his time fitting Molly and Cole with lightly used skates offering good ankle support, and found a well-used and abused pair of adult hockey skates for Ethan, as well.

A mother and her son were shopping at the same time. "If you're going to skate at the town square, you should know that helmets are mandatory," she said with a kindly smile. She showed him the red, white and blue helmet in her shopping basket.

He returned her smile. "Thanks."

"I'm Margaret. And this is my son Trevor. I'd guess he's about the same age as your daughter—sixth grade?"

The kid looked like one of the overly cute boy-band singers Ethan had once glimpsed on television. Apparently even Molly thought he was cute because she blushed a furious shade of red and looked away, clearly mortified.

"She's my niece. And, yes, she's in sixth," Ethan confirmed. "Molly and her brother are from Dallas and just started school today."

From the anguished sound Molly made, it seemed as if she wished Ethan would drop dead and the boy would disappear before she imploded from embarrassment.

"Well, that's real nice," the woman said, apparently oblivious to Molly's groan. "I love your familiar accents. We moved up from Oklahoma two years ago, so your kids and mine have your Southern roots in common. Maybe y'all will have some classes together."

The boy tipped his head and looked Molly over. "I saw you in Stone's math class, and maybe English. I can't believe I got Stone—I was really hoping I would."

Molly lifted her chin a few millimeters, but didn't quite meet his gaze. "I heard she's really awful."

He grinned. "Only if you don't try. She's actually

way cool. She skydives and stuff like that. Sometimes she tells us about it in class."

His mom touched his shoulder and tipped her head toward the cash register. "Trevor's dad is waiting in the car, so we need to get going. Nice to meet you."

Molly surreptitiously watched them leave, her eyes filled with awe. She let out a deep breath.

"So, looks like you made a friend," Ethan murmured. "Maybe you'll see him again at the ice rink or in school."

"Uncle Ethan!" But her mortified tone certainly didn't jibe with the glow in her starstruck eyes.

Chapter Ten

Hannah texted Ethan at five o'clock. When he didn't answer, she tried again at five thirty and at a quarter of six.

Then she began to worry.

The past three hours had been hectic and tense. Frantic family members poured into the hospital and milled around the waiting room and hallway, desperately waiting for news about the three accident victims still in the Aspen Creek ER and those who had been airlifted.

Now that it was all over, Hannah zipped her coat and hurried to her SUV. After turning the key she waited a few minutes for it to warm up.

It had been almost three hours since the kids had gotten out of school, but there'd been no word from Ethan beyond a brief text telling her he'd successfully picked them up. Had he taken them to her house?

The other possibility made her stomach clench.

What if he'd taken off with them for Texas, and planned to petition the court with his urgent need to take over their custody?

She could call the sheriff, report them missing, but were they, really? With the SUV's ubiquitous Minnesota plates and not knowing the license plate number, finding that vehicle in the Wisconsin-Minnesota area would be like finding the proverbial needle in a haystack.

Her pulse pounding, she pressed her gloved fingertips against her temples, willing away the beginnings of a headache. *Please, Lord, let them all be here in town. Please.*

She shifted into Drive and headed slowly toward Main Street, searching the parked cars on either side of the street near the cafés and restaurants. Nothing. Not even near the malt shop, or the busy town square, where she could see a colorful crowd gliding on the ice rink or...

She blinked. Circled the square again. Then began checking the dimly lit side-street parking surrounding the square while trying to call Ethan's phone.

Her breath caught. There it was. A silver SUV, Minnesota plates. She veered to the side of the street, double parked and hurried to the vehicle. Sure enough, Molly and Cole's backpacks were inside.

Relief made her knees weaken, followed by a surge of anger at Ethan's thoughtlessness. He should have responded to her texts. She was the children's guardian and he had no right to...

Be thankful, a still, small voice whispered. *They're here, and they are safe.*

She took a steadying breath. Parked her SUV in the first empty spot she found and then strode toward the ice rink.

Safe or not, Ethan had definitely illustrated that he was still careless and irresponsible, no better than he'd been thirteen years ago. And once again she would learn her lesson well.

* * *

"Uh, oh." Wobbling on his skates, Cole tugged on Ethan's sleeve. "Are we in trouble? Hannah's coming and she looks *mad*."

Ethan held Cole's other hand and steadied him. It took just a second to find Hannah in the crowd. Her long blond hair swung with each purposeful stride as she approached the four-foot-high wooden wall surrounding the ice rink. And yes, indeed—she definitely didn't look happy.

"We'd better go see what she wants, buddy. Ready?" Ethan glided slowly across the rink with Cole in tow.

Molly was still clinging to the fence off to one side, awkward as a scarecrow on her skates. But a girl in a purple coat was talking to her now and gesturing toward the center of the rink.

Molly let go of the fence and reached for the girl's arm but flailed wildly, her feet going in opposite directions. She lurched forward to grab the fence, missed and landed on her rear.

But instead of scowling, she was grinning at the other girl. *Grinning.* Ethan did a double take. That glimpse of her smile made every bump and bruise and penny of this adventure worthwhile, along with the aching muscles and tendons he'd have tomorrow.

Except now Hannah had reached the rink fence, her mouth flattened in a grim line and her eyes flashing fire.

Ethan continued toward her slowly, thankful Cole was with him. She seemed to be upset, but surely she wouldn't make a big scene in front of Cole and so many townspeople whom she probably knew.

"Why didn't you answer my texts?" she demanded in a low voice. "I've been frantic."

Surprised, he raised an eyebrow. "You asked me to pick up the kids and I did."

"But now it's after six o'clock. And I had no idea where you were." Her eyes narrowed. "It didn't cross your mind to let me know?"

Yep, she was angry, all right, but he could also see the worry in her eyes. Had anyone ever been that concerned about Rob and him?

All around him, he could see parents hovering over their kids, watchful of every step. Consoling the little ones who fell, cheering on every tiny success.

It was like watching the old sitcom reruns where the loving mom always wore pearls, heels and a ruffled apron, and the dad dispensed calm, sage advice from a favorite chair. He'd watched those shows as a kid with longing, mystified by a world so different from his own.

He could remember Dad as irritable and impatient over his unexpected role as a single dad after mom left. Gramps wasn't much better. Rob and he had mostly experienced an unstable childhood of changes beyond their control.

He jerked his thoughts back to the present. "I did text, and told you I'd picked them up. I don't have a key to your house, so I called the ER to leave a message for you, wondering if you usually leave a key hidden somewhere. The guy who answered sounded pretty stressed out. He said you were assisting in surgery and couldn't be interrupted. He said he'd give you the message."

"I never got it. But I've been trying to text you and you never answered. Not once."

"My phone is in the SUV, hooked up to the charger. But it only charges if the vehicle is running, so it's still basically dead."

Her agitation seemed to fade. "Where have you been?"

"After I got the kids, we went to get pony food, then to the malt shop. After that, we bought skates, where I think Molly fell for a cute guy from her math class, then we came here. Where, if you take a look to the right, you'll see that Molly is making a new friend. I think. Unless she crashes and nails the poor girl again with her skate blades."

Hannah's steely expression softened. "She needs a friend so much. I'm sorry, Ethan. I was terrified that something had happened."

He eased closer to the fence. "You mean you were terrified that I might have taken the kids. A rather surprising lack of trust, if you ask me."

She looked away, a delicate rose tint blooming on her cheekbones. "It's been a stressful day, in a lot of ways. I apologize for thinking the worst, when you were doing such a good job with them. I was just so worried."

"On that note, I didn't have a key, so your dogs have been in the house since ten this morning. I can finish up here and drop the kids off, if you want to get home to take care of things there."

"I hate to have you make the trip, but that would be super—oh, look!"

He followed her gaze to the far side of the rink where Molly was clinging to her new friend's arm as they slowly, painfully, made their way along the ice. Molly's knees buckled and she went down, but the girl patiently offered her hand and Molly quickly scrambled back to her feet.

"Believe it or not," Ethan drawled, "it's going a lot better."

"Me, too," Cole chirped, his cheeks ruddy from the cold. "I'm better. Let go, Uncle Ethan."

Cole edged onto the ice with a wide-legged stance, moving his skates with tiny forward-and-back scissor motions that gained him little progress. "See?" He looked over his shoulder. "I can stand up!"

Hannah cheered. "Wonderful! I'm so proud of you."

"I haven't been the best teacher, but I saw a sign offering lessons. That might help." Ethan grinned.

Looking up at him, she rested a hand on his. "Great idea. I'll definitely check it out. Thanks again, Ethan, for everything. I'm going to make a quick stop at the grocery store and then be on my way home."

"We'll be there as soon as I can round them up, though it might take a while." But Molly's new friend was nowhere to be seen and Cole was trying to pick himself off the ice.

So maybe it wouldn't take as long as he thought.

Hannah parked in front of her garage just as Ethan's headlights swung into the driveway. When none of his car doors opened, she went to the front driver's-side door and rapped lightly on the window.

He rolled the window partway down. "We'll be in— just give us a minute."

"Something wrong?" She peered in the backseat window, where Cole appeared to be pouting and Molly wore a scowl. She stepped back to Ethan's window. "Oh, dear."

He nodded. "We've been talking about people who are friends and those who aren't. And how you can't really make others play nice."

"So…something happened at the ice rink?"

Ethan nodded. "The girl who befriended Molly

pretty much stabbed her in the back as soon as some other girls came out on the ice." He looked at the rearview mirror. "Right, Molly? She wasn't kind at all. But I promise you, you'll meet nice people before long."

"I hate it here," Molly burst out. "Those girls were *laughing* at me. And the kids at school are all *mean*. They hate me, and say I talk like a stupid cowboy. I'm not going back there. Not ever."

"I love your Texas accent, sweetie," Hannah said. "And others will, too. I think it makes you very cool."

Molly didn't budge.

"I don't blame you for feeling upset, but let's go into the house, okay? It's cold out here and we can talk later." Hannah opened Cole's door and helped him out, then grabbed the ice skates that were on the floor.

Ethan went to the back of his SUV and carried a fifty-pound sack of horse feed into the garage, then retrieved her groceries from the backseat of the Subaru and carried them into the house, with Cole on his heels.

Molly still sat in the backseat, her face filled with misery.

"Honey, I know you're upset. But please come inside, okay? You're going to get really cold out here."

At the sound of a faint, pitiful whimper, Hannah straightened and looked around the yard. "Do you hear something?"

Molly's scowl deepened and she sunk lower in her seat. But then she must have heard it, too, because she straightened and looked out her window.

The overcast sky cast only a faint glow over the heavy drifts of snow in the yard and the high banks the snowplow had left along each side of the road.

"That sound didn't come from the house or garage,"

Hannah said quietly. "It sounds to me like something is hurt."

Molly got out of the car and joined her as she scanned the yard. "There—" She pointed to the base of the metal flagpole by the garage. "What is it?"

She hurried toward the small, quivering shape.

"No, Molly. Stay back," Hannah called out sharply as she went after the girl.

Now she could make out the shape—a skeletal dog of some kind that had been chained to the flagpole while they were away. Chained outside in the snow. With no shelter, in rapidly dropped temperatures.

"Don't get too close. She's terrified and she might bite."

But Molly ignored her and crouched, murmuring gentle words. Still, the dog cowered as far away from her as the chain allowed, its tail tucked between its legs.

Molly lifted tear-filled eyes to Hannah. "Just *look* at her. She's all bones, and there's something weird about her neck—it looks crusty. What if we hadn't come back tonight? She would have frozen to death out here. Who would do such a terrible thing?"

Far too many horrible people, Hannah thought. Molly's tender heart hadn't yet encountered the wretched people who locked dogs away in dirty kennels and never let them out, or kept them on chains in miserable conditions.

Which was exactly why Hannah had begun her private, no-kill rescue. "The one good thing is that someone cared enough to bring her here, where she'll now have a chance."

"W-will she be okay?"

"I'm going to get some treats for her and hope to make friends before we try to move her inside."

But Molly was already edging closer to the stray, oblivious to the risk of approaching a dog this scared. Her sympathy would doubtless overcome all caution if she was left for even a minute without adult supervision.

"On second thought—can *you* go get a little stainless-steel food pan, put some kibble in it and bring it to me? And switch on the outside floodlights when you come back out."

Molly raced into the garage and returned in a flash with an overflowing food pan. "What do I do—should I put it down in front of her?"

"No. Come over here behind me and let's see if this works."

Hannah crouched and tossed a piece of kibble a couple feet in front of the dog. The animal yelped and fought the chain, but she was already at its end and had no escape. When she settled, her bony sides were heaving and she was wobbling on her feet.

"That's a good pup," Hannah murmured in a gentle, soothing voice. "You'll be glad to come inside. Yes, you will. A nice warm bed, doggie friends, good food."

She tossed more kibble, and this time the poor thing just quivered. Then she edged forward with her head down and ears flattened. She gave Hannah a long, wary look, then suspiciously sniffed at the kibble before wolfing it down.

"Can she sleep in my room tonight?" Molly whispered. "Please?"

"Not yet. I think she's been injured. She's scared. Just coming into the garage would be a big transition right now. She might not be accustomed to any sort of indoor shelter."

"But she's so cold," Molly pleaded. "Look at her shaking."

"The garage is heated. I just keep the temp low so the transition of the animals going outside isn't so abrupt." Hannah tossed more kibble, a few inches closer to her own feet. The dog took a half step closer and eyed the food. Then she backed up.

"She's probably shaking from fear as well as hypothermia. The poor girl doesn't have any body fat at all and I hate to think what I'll find under that wet, matted coat."

"Can you take care of...of whatever is wrong?"

"I'm going to talk to the vet in the morning and see if I can take her in for an exam before I go to work."

"It's so cool that you do this." Molly looked at Hannah with newfound respect. "But how will you get her there? She looks so scared."

"If she's too frightened to be lured into my car, I'll see if the vet can stop by. I don't want to waste any time if she needs antibiotics or other treatment, and I very much doubt she's had any vaccinations. I also need her checked for an identification chip."

Molly rocked back on her heels, aghast. "Why?"

"She could have been stolen from a good home and then mistreated, or maybe she ran away from nice owners and got lost, then fell into the wrong hands. There might be children who miss her terribly. Or, sadly, maybe it was her real owner who is responsible for this."

Molly's eyes widened with horror and started to fill with tears.

"You should probably go inside," Hannah said quickly. "Take your bath and get your pajamas on. You must be cold out here."

Molly shook her head. "No. I'm staying."

"Just a few more minutes then." Hannah tossed another piece of kibble and this time the dog crept cautiously forward on its belly to within a few feet of them. She nabbed the morsel and didn't retreat.

"What a good girl you are," Hannah crooned in a soft, low voice. "You'll be so pretty when you put on a few pounds and have a nice bath. Where have you been to end up looking like this?"

"What should we call her, Aunt Hannah? She can't just be 'the dog.'"

Hannah glanced at her and smiled. "Since you were the one who found her, I think you should decide."

"Belle."

"From the cartoon?"

Molly shook her head firmly. "Because she is going to be beautiful. I just know it."

"Perfect. Then Belle it is."

After another ten minutes of patience, the dog finally edged forward enough to sniff Hannah's hand. Another fifteen and she finally accepted gentle strokes against the side of her head, though her tail was still clamped between her back legs and the hair along her spine raised.

"Molly, can you do me a favor? I've got her distracted right now. Can you give us a wide berth and slowly, quietly, unfasten the chain from the flagpole? Then bring that end to me. Try to not let it jingle too much."

After taking care of the chain, Molly watched with rapt attention as Hannah slowly eased the frightened dog into the garage and offered her a pan of water.

The chickens were already roosting for the night and didn't stir, but Lucy barked once, then looked over the fence surrounding her pen at the newcomer with frank curiosity. Once the garage door was shut, Hannah breathed a sigh of relief.

Whatever happened now, at least the poor thing couldn't panic and escape into the cold winter night.

"Now I need to fix a big pen for her, with lots of blankets, and she'll be comfy for the night. And I also need to put the other dogs out one last time. So, young lady," Hannah said firmly, though she couldn't quite contain a smile. "You've been a great help, but now it's almost nine o'clock and this time I mean it. Go get ready for bed. I'll be in shortly, so we can talk about your tough day at school."

Chapter Eleven

When Hannah finally finished her chores outside, she walked into the house and found Ethan on the living room floor, where he and Cole were playing yet another game of Candy Land.

"I figured you and Molly were busy outside, so I thought I'd better stay with Cole until you came in," Ethan said as he stood. "I wasn't sure what to do about bath time, though, so I just let him get into his pajamas. He's also had a bedtime snack, and just a couple minutes ago he brushed his teeth. Molly is taking a shower."

"Wow. Thank so much, Ethan. I appreciate it." She smiled down at Cole. "So, let's go read some stories, all right? Just a few, though. I should have been in an hour ago to get you to bed. Sorry."

"I had fun with Uncle Ethan. You can go back outside if you want, 'cause we're playing a game."

"You'll have to finish another time. Can you say good-night to your uncle?"

Cole hesitated, then stood and plowed into Ethan and wrapped his arms around Ethan's good leg. "Thanks! Come again, okay? *Someday* you're gonna win."

"I doubt that. You are way too good." Ethan ruffled

the boy's hair and let his hand linger, as if he were savoring a moment he didn't want to end. "Sleep tight, okay?"

Hannah walked into Cole's room and flipped on the light. She gasped. "Ethan—did you do this?"

He sauntered into the room. "I hope it's all right. I didn't want to think about Cole using a mattress on the floor again, so he and I studied the situation while you were outside. Is it all right?"

"All right? It's perfect. Thank you so much."

He shrugged. "It was pretty easy. We switched some of the pieces so he has a regular twin bed now, and the spare pieces are in the upstairs storeroom in case you want to switch things back again."

Overcome with the sudden temptation to give him a kiss of thanks on the cheek, she took a quick step back, knowing it might unleash a flood of emotions she could not afford. The children were all that mattered right now. "It's wonderful. Absolutely wonderful."

"I like it, too," Cole said, climbing under the covers. "I'm not so high up, in case I have to go to the bathroom. And Maisie can even be on my bed, see?" The dog, curled up at the foot of the bed, thumped her tail once at the sound of her name.

"This is perfect in every way," Hannah said, her heart overflowing with love for this sweet little boy. And with sadness, too. Dee had missed so much of her children's lives already. "Let's say our prayers now, okay? And then we'd better let you get a good night's sleep."

Cole dutifully recited his prayers. She kissed him good-night, turned on his night-light and went out to the living room, where Ethan was pensively staring into the fire he'd started earlier, his thumbs hooked in his back jeans' pockets.

"Molly is done in the shower and back in her room," he said in a low voice. "She looks pretty tired."

"I'm not surprised. Now, for the tricky part," Hannah said quietly. "Convincing her to go back to school tomorrow. And waiting for more night terrors—or not. I'll be praying that Cole will be all right."

"I was just heading out, but do you want me to stay a while longer?" he asked with a self-deprecating smile. "Not that I have any experience with either problem, but I could offer moral support."

"We'll manage. Could I offer you a cup of decaf or cocoa for the road?" she asked lightly. "Or leftover turkey? I'd be very happy to send some with you if you have a fridge."

"I've got just a tiny fridge, so I think I'll pass. Thanks, though." He reached for an envelope on the mantel and handed it to her. "This was taped to your front door when we all got home. Addressed to you, of course."

She slid a finger under the flap and withdrew a single sheet of paper. "Apparently the fire chief—who is also the local fire inspector—came out today. This is the report I can give to the insurance company."

"What did he decide?"

"Molly will be so glad to hear this. She was worried that the fire was her fault, because she had moved the chicken's panel heater. But Bill figures it was an electrical short at the other end of the barn. Frayed wires, probably thanks to mice."

"So you shouldn't have any issues with the insurance coverage."

"I don't think so. It should just be a matter of getting

the check and waiting for warm enough weather to start building another small barn." She paced the length of the living room then turned back. "I've had to make do with that old building, but this time, I want to work on plans and make it right. Clean, spacious, bright, with better exercise runs, for starters."

"A facility like that would cost many times what you'll get from your insurance claim."

"But it would be a start, anyway." She thought for a moment. "I'll have to talk to the other women who run home-based rescues like mine. Maybe we can try once again to stir up interest for a permanent shelter in town. Get the city council involved. Fund-raise and all that."

He smiled. "I believe you have more energy than anyone I ever met."

She laughed at that. "Energy, but not a whole lot of money. And I'm afraid I have an enemy on the city council. But it doesn't hurt to dream, right?"

Something sad flashed in his eyes. "No, I guess not."

She walked him to the front door. "Thanks again for taking the kids this afternoon. I have friends I could've called, but I didn't know if Molly and Cole would be comfortable with anyone except you. Not yet."

He lifted a shoulder dismissively. "No problem. They're why I'm in Wisconsin, and I'm glad to be with them any time I can. Never hesitate to ask."

"About that…" She bit her lower lip. "I wonder if I could ask you for another favor?"

"What do you need?"

"That new dog needs a ride to the vet clinic tomorrow morning. I called Darcy—the vet—tonight on her cell, and she said she could fit us in at nine, but I have appointments starting at nine. I hate to wait till the weekend."

"No problem. Anything else?"

"Maybe. I don't know when it might happen, but there might be an inspection of my rescue facilities sometime soon. The inspector probably won't give me any advance warning, but when he arrives he'll need access to my garage. So at some point, if I can't get away from the clinic, I might need to ask you to go unlock it for him."

"No problem with that, either."

"Super. I'll show you where the spare key is. And, Ethan…I'm sorry I was so testy about where you were with the kids. I never should have assumed…"

"It's been a long time since we were together, Hannah, and we no longer know each other that well. People change. And it's no secret that our goals are polar opposites when it comes to the kids."

"Still…"

"No, your first priority is them, and that's how it should be," he said gravely. "So I'd say you were simply acting on instinct to keep them safe."

"But I didn't mean to—"

He cut her off. "Don't overthink this, Hannah. Just forget it."

Their eyes met. Locked. And then he gave her a faint, sad smile. "I've made mistakes in my life. A lot of them. But the more I'm here, the more I realize that my worst one was when I let you go."

He'd imagined himself doing any number of things on Tuesday while the kids were in school and Hannah was working at the health clinic.

Holding the leash of an emaciated, cowering dog and feeling the glares of the other three clients in a vet's waiting room was not one of them.

They had a right to look outraged at Belle's condition. He felt exactly the same way. But if they only knew how long it had taken him to beg and cajole this dog from her pen to his car, they'd be awarding him a medal.

As it was, he was pretty sure the lady in the corner chair, with a Westie as white and pristine as fresh snow, was surreptitiously calling the cops to have him arrested for animal abuse.

"Come here, sweet girl," he murmured. Belle was at the end of her leash, under the chair, as if she expected him to attack at any moment. She clearly wasn't planning to budge.

The judgmental stares aside, he'd felt his heart clench painfully at his first good view of her this morning. Her bony frame and the open sores on every bony prominence made him long to make her last owner regret he'd ever been born. What kind of person could do something like this to a helpless dog?

"Mr. Williams?" A young woman in a pink uniform with KayCee on her name badge appeared in the doorway leading to the exam rooms. Her jaw dropped. "Oh, my goodness. Hannah called and told us about this one. But I never…" She took a deep breath. "Will she lead?"

"Not really. I can only get her to move along with bits of turkey." He gave the girl a wry smile. "Hannah just happened to have some leftovers, and I figured it was important to get her here one way or another."

"Let me try." She took the leash from him and crooned to Belle. She reached under the chair to pet her head, but the dog jerked back in abject fear.

Ethan offered her the Ziploc bag of tiny bits of turkey. "This works better. I promise."

"I read that turkey is toxic to dogs," the woman with the Westie announced, her eyes narrowed.

KayCee tipped her head toward an array of handouts on one of the end tables. "Turkey skin and fat can cause pancreatitis in dogs, and they can choke on the bones. But our vet says a little bit of the white meat is okay."

Ethan felt the glares of the other clients boring into his back as he, Belle and the vet tech slowly made their way down the hall, though by now Belle had planted her butt on the floor and was leaning back with all her might as she was being towed toward an alcove with a scale.

She feebly resisted before stepping onto the platform. The digital screen read 24.4 pounds.

"That can't be good," Ethan muttered.

The girl jotted the results on her clipboard. She ushered them into the next exam room. "Dr. Leighton will be in shortly. Just have a seat."

Here, amid the scent of sanitizer and the barking of dogs from somewhere in the back of the building, Belle seemed to decide Ethan was her only ally in this frightening place.

She pressed her bony side tightly against his leg, her breathing fast and shallow and her head bowed in abject defeat. He ran his hand lightly along her back in long, slow strokes, then began rubbing gently behind her ears.

"What a good girl you are," he soothed. "In no time at all, you'll be romping with those other dogs at Hannah's place and sleeping on someone's bed."

Molly's, he guessed. When Hannah had called him this morning about the vet appointment, she'd said that she'd found Molly out in the garage this morning, curled up by the dog's pen.

A thirtysomething woman in a lab coat, with shiny brown hair twisted into a knot on the top of her head, stepped into the room.

"Goodness," she exclaimed as she surveyed the quivering dog. "Where have you been, poor thing?"

"Did Hannah explain when she called?"

"Yes, she did." The woman extended her hand. "Dr. Leighton. You must be Ethan?"

He nodded.

"And this must be Belle." She crouched and offered the back of her hand for Belle to consider, then ran gentle hands over the dog's emaciated frame. Whining, Belle cringed under her touch.

"She looks like she might be a springer spaniel cross, maybe with some shepherd in the mix. Without doing a DNA test, we can't really be sure, but that doesn't matter. She's a good twenty pounds under weight and if she'd gone much longer she would've gone into irreversible organ failure."

"Can you write down what she should be eating?"

The vet nodded. "Hannah has been through this before, but yes—I'll send home instructions."

"And those awful sores on her neck and hips?"

"Looks like her choke chain collar was too tight and became imbedded in her neck, and those are pressure sores over her hip bones. She must have been chained someplace where she had little or no bedding and hardly any space to move. Terrible."

Ethan winced. "Also, Hannah wants you to check for an identification chip."

"The tech can do that in a bit. In fact, we need to keep Belle for a few days. That collar has to be surgically removed. Believe it or not, she's a young dog. I'd guess around two." Dr. Leighton shook her head firmly. "Everything you see can be fixed. She deserves a far better life, and Hannah and I are going to make sure she gets it."

As if Belle understood the vet's tone and body language, if not the words, her tail began to slowly wag.

Ethan watched as the vet continued her exam, and realized he was learning about more than just Leighton's caring attitude.

His stay in Wisconsin was also revealing just how much he had misjudged Hannah all those years ago.

From choosing a challenging career where she could help people every single day, to her dedication to saving abused and abandoned animals, the depths of Hannah's own compassionate heart were far greater than he ever would have guessed.

Coupled with her love and protectiveness toward the children, he now knew she'd be a formidable opponent indeed, if their custody battle ended up in a court of law.

Chapter Twelve

Molly trudged out to Hannah's Subaru, her trademark sulk firmly in place. She joined Cole in the backseat without a word.

"So, how was your second day at school?"

"I hate this place and I want to go home. To *Texas*."

Was that what she truly wanted? Would she really be happier living with Ethan, after all—or was she simply longing for the days before her parents died?

The children's happiness was paramount, but there were so many uncertainties in that equation that Hannah didn't even want to think about it. Not yet.

Molly had fallen asleep last night before Hannah had made it to her bedroom, so there had been no chance for a much-needed discussion. And with the return of Cole's night terrors, Molly had awakened in the middle of the night, and then tossed and turned.

Lack of sleep hadn't made the child's day any better.

Molly picked at a loose thread on her backpack strap. "How is Belle?"

"She's at the vet clinic right now."

Molly jerked upright, her eyes wide with alarm. "They wouldn't— They couldn't—"

"They're taking good care of her, I promise. They're giving her IV fluids and antibiotics, and they've started treating the ulcers."

"I don't believe you. Maybe they'll decide to put her to sleep." Molly's lower lip trembled. "I want to see her. Can we go there? Right now?"

"That happened with our kitty," Cole mumbled. "She went to the vet and never came back."

Oh, dear. Hannah turned her SUV toward the vet clinic. "I'm so sorry to hear that, Cole. Was she very old and sick?"

Cole shook his head. "She couldn't come to our new 'partment so Dad sent her to heaven."

Instead of a shelter? Hannah had a feeling there was more to the story, but maybe Dee just hadn't explained it very well.

"There might have been a very good reason, sweetie. Sometime animals are suffering too much, and it's more kind to let them go."

"No," Cole insisted with a stubborn shake of his head. "She couldn't come to the 'partment when we moved. It wasn't fair."

If he was right, Hannah totally agreed. "Well, just to show you that Belle is receiving good care, we're going to the clinic. Okay? It's just a few blocks away."

Molly and Cole sat silently in the backseat until Hannah pulled into the parking lot, but they both beat her into the clinic.

Hannah followed them inside. "I have a couple of kids here who are worried about Belle—the dog I sent in this morning. Can we see her?"

Marilyn, the sixtysomething receptionist, shook her head. "I'm sorry—"

"No!" Molly screamed. "You *killed* her?"

"Of course not," Marilyn said gently. "The vet is doing some surgery on her right now, but she should be fine."

Molly looked up at Hannah with a stricken expression. "I want to see her," she begged. "*Please*. What if she dies? I didn't even get to say goodbye."

This wasn't just about the dog, Molly realized with a pang of sorrow. It was about life and loss and grief that had to weigh on these kids every single day.

The parents they loved had left one day and never returned. How did a child ever recover from that?

"About how long until Belle is finished?"

"Maybe a half hour, but I'm not sure." Marilyn lowered her voice. "Darcy made sure it was the last appointment of the day, just in case it took longer. Imbedded choke chain. Deep."

Hannah swallowed hard then summoned a cheery smile. "Okay, kids, it's going to be a long while, and even then Belle will need to recover from anesthesia. Let's walk down Main Street."

"I want to stay." Molly plopped down on the nearest chair.

"Molly, there's nothing to do here, and it will be a long wait. Why don't we check out Keeley's cookies at her antiques store, then we can stop at the Christmas Shoppe. I'd like you both to pick out some new decorations for our Christmas tree so we can go out and cut our tree tomorrow. By then it will be time to come back and see Belle."

Feeling as if she were being followed by two reluctant ducklings, Hannah headed down Main Street. The sky was overcast with the feeling of snow in the air and dusk was falling earlier every passing day. All of the storefronts were decorated and brightly lit. Overhead, Christmas lights were twinkling on every lamppost.

At Keeley's store, the stained-glass lamps and sparkling antique chandeliers inside cast a welcoming glow onto the sidewalk. Hannah ushered the kids into the store. "This is where your pretty stained-glass bedside lamp came from, Molly. Keeley gave it to you as a gift."

Molly nodded.

From behind the cash register Keeley waved and pointed to the table with a coffeemaker, a pitcher of ice water and an array of decorated Christmas cookies on a crystal platter covered with a glass dome, then continued to wait on a customer.

"I don't suppose this would be your favorite kind of store, Cole. But would you like to look around or would you rather sit at the ice-cream table by the window and have your cookies?"

Cole zoomed to the window and settled on a wrought-iron chair. He looked up in awe at a vintage lamp with cartoon figures chasing each other around the rim of the shade.

After wandering aimlessly through the store, Molly joined her brother, her gaze fixed on a two-foot Christmas tree adorned with antique decorations in the corner. The sadness in her eyes was palpable.

"I love Christmas," Hannah said as she brought over the platter and two paper plates.

Cole tentatively picked a Santa cookie and looked up at her.

"Aren't these pretty? I'm sure it's okay if you want two."

Molly halfheartedly picked the cookie closest to her on the platter. Her gaze veered back to the tree. "It's not like Christmas this year," she said softly. "Not the same at all."

Hannah set the platter back on the serving table and brought over two waters and a black coffee. "I don't suppose it will be. But we will always have Christmas. Every year, we celebrate the birth of the Christ child, just as you did before, and that will never, ever, change. I promise. And every year, we'll have presents under a tree and Christmas stockings. And I hope we can talk about your Christmas memories—and try to make new ones, too."

"We had a tree in a box," Cole announced.

"An artificial tree then. I'll bet it was nice."

He nodded. "And we had favorite decorations—ones we made at school. One had my picture on it from preschool."

Hannah's eyes started to burn. The shipping boxes from Texas weren't all emptied yet—just the ones with the children's clothes, toys and books. The others were stored away in the bedroom upstairs. But she'd looked inside each one and knew for a fact that none of them had contained Christmas ornaments.

Cynthia had probably seen it all as rubbish and discarded it. And in the process, she'd destroyed one more connection the kids could have had with their past.

"After your cookies, we're going to buy some Christmas ornaments, and those will be yours forever. But do you know what? I'd love it if we could make some, too. Those would be so special—and we could do it every year."

"Hey, guys." Keeley sauntered over and pulled up a fourth chair to join them. "I'm so glad you stopped in. How's everything going?"

Cole shyly ducked his head. Molly traced her finger across her cookie and didn't look up.

"I am so thrilled to have these two with me," Hannah said. "I hope I can find lots of fun things for them to do. Any ideas?"

"Let me think. You've been on a sleigh ride?"

"But it had wheels," Cole said, taking another bite of his cookie.

"Then that's what you should do, now that we have snow. It's only a few days until the weekend and the sleigh rides start again." Keeley worried at her lower lip with her teeth, thinking. "The kids at church will be caroling that night, too, as they walk down Main Street. Have you two met any of the kids at church yet?"

Hannah shook her head. "They haven't. We were snowed in Sunday morning, unfortunately. Mingling with those kids would've made this first week at school easier, I think. But maybe we'll run into some of them at the Advent service on Wednesday."

Molly eyes widened in alarm. "You aren't going to, like, make me *talk* to them. Right?"

"That would be awful, no doubt." Hannah hid a smile. "But if you see someone from school who looks kinda nice, you might ask a question about school, or about the youth group at church or about what they like to do around here for fun."

"Sounds like a good plan," Keeley agreed. "Even adults find it hard to meet people in a new town, and if you don't try, it can be very lonely."

"Lots of people have moved here during the last few years," Hannah added. "Did you know Keeley's fiancé is from Texas like you are?" At Cole's sudden attention, she nodded. "And Connor is a real cowboy. Now he trains and shows horses here in Wisconsin, but he grew up on a ranch out West. When the weather is nicer, maybe we can go out to the horse ranch where he works, so you can ride."

Even Molly perked up at that. *"Really?"*

"Absolutely. But right now we'd better scoot over to the Christmas Shoppe, so we can get back to the vet clinic before it closes. Thank Keeley for the lovely cookies and we can be on our way."

Cole and Molly bundled up into their coats and mittens, dutifully murmured their thanks and went out to the sidewalk.

Hannah hesitated at the door and looked back. "Thanks, Keel."

Keeley joined her at the entryway and they both looked out the front window at the children running their hands over the snow-frosted bench just outside. "So how are things going—really?"

"They're still grieving, of course. And I knew moving here wouldn't be easy. But sometimes…" Hannah felt tears start burning in her eyes, but she willed them away. "Sometimes they say or do something that rips my heart in pieces. We were just at the vet clinic, and Molly…"

Hannah swallowed hard, unable to go on for a moment. "Can you imagine the pain of losing your parents and having no chance to say goodbye? How can they ever recover from that?"

Keeley gave Hannah a brief, comforting hug. "You will just keep loving them, Hannah. Make them feel loved, and safe, and honor their memories. Do you remember the funeral for the Jones' boy a few years ago?"

"I'll never forget it."

"I remember his distraught mom asking us how she could ever get through her grief and you said…"

Hannah managed a wobbly smile. "By holding on to the faith that he was already with the Lord in heaven, beyond all suffering, and that she would be with him again."

"You'll all get through this in time. I promise. There isn't another person who could handle the challenges better than you will."

Impatient now, the kids were both looking through the front window at her, their hands framing their faces as they peered through the breath-frosted glass.

Hannah felt her heart warm and give an extra little thump. "I'll be praying every single day that you're right, Keel. Because nothing matters to me more."

Hannah had envisioned a long and careful search through the Christmas Shoppe while Molly and Cole searched for their perfect ornaments for the tree.

But it took all of five minutes with Molly finding a springer spaniel ornament that looked vaguely like Belle on a display tree right inside the door, and Cole finding a golden retriever one that looked a lot like Maisie on the same tree.

Evening shoppers were beginning to fill the sidewalks as they stepped out of the store, and holiday music filtered into the chilly, early evening air through loudspeakers on the lampposts.

A light dusting of snow had landed over the town, making Hannah feel as if she were walking in an old-fashioned snow globe.

In just a few minutes they were back at the clinic.

Marilyn greeted them with a smile. "I'm glad you made it back. We'll be closing in fifteen minutes."

Molly fidgeted from one foot to the other. "Can we see Belle?"

"Of course you can. Dr. Leighton is gone, but I can take you back there. But you have to promise that you won't touch anything or get too close to the cages. And, especially, do not poke your fingers into the cages trying to pet the animals. We have four post-ops back there, and dogs that are sweet at home can be quite nervous in a vet clinic."

When both kids nodded, she led the way to the back of the clinic. A night-light warmed the darkness with a soft glow.

Three dogs were immediately awake and barking when Marilyn turned on the fluorescent lights. "Your Belle is over here, to the left. The last time I looked in on her she was quite subdued, but she's in poor condition and doesn't have a lot of energy yet. She also took a little longer than usual to wake up after the anesthesia."

Belle was crouched at the back of her cage, her ears flattened and tail tucked when Molly approached.

"She looks so *miserable*," Molly whispered. "I don't think she even remembers me."

"I'm sure she's scared. Here she is, in another new place with strangers, and on some pain meds that might make her a little woozy. I'm sure she's never had an IV drip before, or NG tube feedings. But Dr. Leighton thinks she'll be a lot perkier tomorrow."

"And then we can take her home?"

Marilyn pursed her lips. "That, I couldn't say. I'm sure we'll have a better idea in a day or two. You wouldn't want her home too soon, only to get weak and sick, would you?"

Molly shook her head vigorously. "I want her to be well."

Cole pointed to three dogs in the cages along the back wall. "Why are they here? Are they all sick, too?"

"Let's see. One neuter, one spay. Those two will go home tomorrow. One got away from his owner and was hit by a car, so he had his femur repaired this afternoon."

"I'd like to be a vet someday," Molly murmured, looking around the room with awe.

"Good for you. There's a high percentage of female vets these days." Marilyn ushered them out of the recovery room and switched off the overhead lights. "Study hard, get good grades and take all the math and science classes you can in high school. It will help a lot when you take the pre-vet classes in college."

Molly looked up at Marilyn with shining eyes. "I will. There's nothing in the world I want more."

Hannah checked the new text message on her phone and sighed. Until she'd brought the children north, she'd never hesitated to put in extra hours at work. Every day brought new challenges and she loved both the patients and the staff she worked with.

But now, she just wanted to be home when the kids weren't in school. To that end she'd shortened her clinic hours and asked to be taken off the on-call schedule until after Christmas. But apparently the other PA in town was out sick.

She tapped her phone for Ethan's number. The call went straight to voice mail, so she waited a minute, tried again and left a brief message. Where was he?

She glanced in the rearview mirror as she shifted her vehicle into Drive. Cole slumped in his seat, his face pale and drawn. "Are you all right?"

He nodded, not meeting her gaze in the rearview mirror.

"I guess this was a pretty big day for you two." She turned onto Main Street. "Did you have a good time?"

No one answered.

"I hope you don't mind, but I need to stop by Ethan's cabin to see if he's available tomorrow, just in case I get called back to work. Is that okay with you?"

When neither of them answered, she directed another glance up at the mirror.

Molly glowered back at her. "We don't need a baby-sitter."

"Maybe not, but I don't feel comfortable with you two alone out in the country."

"Mom let us stay home when she went to the store. Nothing happened then."

"Maybe not, but it will make me feel a lot better if there's an adult around." At the other end of town she braked at the four-way stop sign in front of the coffee shop. "Okay?"

"Isn't that his car?" Cole piped up. "Right over there."

Sure enough, it was the SUV with Minnesota plates.

Hannah parked in the next open space, and led the way into the coffee shop. Busy as usual, most of the tables were filled and a number of people were eating at the long lunch counter.

"There he is," Cole chirped, pointing toward the back. "Talking to that pretty lady standing by his booth."

Hannah's heart stumbled.

Dressed in a lipstick-red wool jacket and short skirt, the woman's clothing molded every perfect curve. Glittering diamonds flashed at her ears and wrists. With the four-inch heels of her tall black leather boots and the thick, wavy blonde hair spilling down her back, she looked like she'd just stepped off the cover of *Vogue*.

She was obviously a wealthy young woman, and from the silvery trill of her laughter, she and Ethan were enjoying a delightful conversation. No wonder he hadn't answered Hannah's calls. He had much better things to do.

Forcing back a flare of unexpected jealousy, Hannah glanced down at her own puffy black jacket—the one that probably added twenty pounds to her silhouette, and the khaki slacks badly stained with formula a baby had spit up on her at the clinic.

But jealousy was a ridiculous response.

Ethan and she had no personal relationship. None—beyond the politely adversarial situation they'd been locked in since he'd appeared at her door. He was free to flirt with anyone he chose, and it didn't matter to her at all. And if his taste now ran toward women like this one, he probably thought Hannah was pathetic.

"Uh…Ethan looks like he's busy. Let's go," she murmured.

But Cole was already racing to the booth, with Molly on his heels, so there was no turning back.

The blonde looked down at them with horror, then raised her gaze and gave Hannah a sweeping, dismissive glance. "You have a *family*?" she snapped, turning back to Ethan. Then she spun on her heel and walked out of the coffee shop.

"Boy, she was *mad*, Uncle Ethan," Cole exclaimed as he watched her disappear through the front door. "Was she a movie star or something?"

"She just stopped to visit, I guess."

"Sorry we interrupted," Hannah said dryly. "I can run after her and tell her that you are totally available, if you'd like."

"Please don't."

"Hannah's better, anyway," Molly muttered. "At least she's nice."

Faint praise, but even that much was a surprise and Hannah gave her shoulders a quick, one-armed hug. "We saw your car and stopped, because I tried to call a little while ago."

Ethan gestured at his coffee cup. "Join me?"

"No, I've got to get the kids home, but thanks, anyway. I just learned that I need to be on call tomorrow evening. If I do get called in, can you spend some time with the kids?" She flicked a glance at the front door of the coffee shop. "Unless you'll be seeing your...friend, that is."

He grinned at Molly and Cole. "Nope. Hands down, I'd rather spend time with you two, any day."

"Thanks, Ethan." Hannah waggled an eyebrow up and down. "And just to make sure no one is bored, I have a cool project for the three of you. Just wait and see."

Chapter Thirteen

Ethan had already noticed that Hannah's ten acres held a lot of trees.

What he hadn't noticed was that there was an immeasurable number of pine trees out there, but apparently *none* of them were perfect enough for a Christmas tree.

Cole ran from one tree to the next, studying each one from every angle and then moving on. His standard of perfection was the artificial tree his parents had put up every year, and none of these live ones fit the bill.

No wonder. What self-respecting tree would want to look like a scraggly replica with plastic needles?

Trailing well behind, Molly wanted something "super tall and wide at the bottom" like the one she'd seen on a book cover in the school library.

But it was already five and soon it would be getting dark.

Carrying the saw, Ethan trudged doggedly after them through the deep, pristine snow, his bad leg aching a little more with every step.

He had a feeling Hannah could have found a way to expedite this process, but she'd been called back to the hospital and probably wouldn't be home until seven.

Hannah's "cool project" was proving to be cool in every sense of the word.

She'd asked him to find a Christmas tree with the kids, but every time he tried to take a stand about going no farther into the forest, he was met with wails about this being their very first tree to cut down and it had to be *perfect*.

Good luck with that.

Yet this was the first time he'd seen the kids show any real enthusiasm about their first Christmas without their mom and dad. So how could he deny them anything within his power?

Ethan's knee buckled, sending him face-first into a mound of snow and the boulder hidden beneath that deceptive mantle of white.

Stars exploded in his brain.

He wobbled, dizzy and disoriented as he tried to push off the rock and regain his feet. Now the entire forest seemed be spinning in disjointed loops that dipped and swayed, and sent him careening against the trunk of a tree.

Closing his eyes, he held on to the tree trunk and took slow, deep breaths. Waited to regain his balance.

A flash of motion flickered at the corner of his eye and he pivoted toward it in time to see a magnificent buck with a massive rack not twenty yards away. Regal, the deer took several slow steps with its head held high, then bounded away into the forest.

"Kids," Ethan whispered, "did you see that?"

He pivoted slowly toward where he'd last seen Molly, then to where Cole had been just a moment ago.

Both of them were gone.

"Molly! Cole!"

The forest remained dead silent. Even the breeze had gone still.

He resolutely changed course toward the last place he'd seen Cole, slipping on unseen, downed tree trunks hidden under mounds of snow, stumbling over rocks.

At the top of a small rise he finally connected with Cole's boot prints, which headed off to the west and a rugged hill covered with thickets of low, thorny branches.

Now his heart was beating double-time, as much from worry as the exertion of plowing through deep snow. Where on earth had the boy gone?

"Cole! Molly!" He waited. Listened. Then continued onward. In less than an hour it would be too dark to see the tracks.

He briefly closed his eyes, remembering all of the times he'd been desperate—trying to reach a wounded buddy under fire. Searching through a bombed-out city of rubble and despair, determined to take out any snipers before they got to him and his men first.

God hadn't ever answered his prayers then and after a while he'd given up.

But now, with two kids missing and a below-freezing night ahead, he dredged up those rusty words and began to pray. *Please, God, I know I'm not worthy. But please, please help me find those two innocent kids—they don't deserve to die out here.*

Then he struck out again, scanning the terrain for any sign of the kids as he went.

The tracks were veering south, thank goodness, in the general direction of Hannah's house. And there were Molly's tracks, too.

But why would they have turned back without a word? Or had they? When he looked down again, the tracks had vanished. Had that buck been a figment of his imagination, too?

Scrubbing a hand over his face, he stared in wonder at the blood on his glove and tried to sort through his thoughts. Figure out where he'd gone wrong.

But he couldn't remember a thing.

Hannah searched the house then looked out into the backyard.

Ethan's SUV was in the driveway, the house unlocked. But none of the lights had been turned on against the approaching darkness, so maybe they were still outside, dragging a pine tree behind them like a caveman's trophy kill.

She smiled to herself, wondering how long that decision had taken. She'd told Ethan to stay within the fenced border of her property just for that very reason.

It was all too easy to be lured farther and farther into the forest by the prospect of a perfect tree waiting just out of reach, and then become confused and lost—especially at dusk. But if he'd followed directions, he and the kids would always run into her fence line sooner or later and be able to find their way home.

Shoving her feet into her snow boots, she shrugged into her heavy down jacket, pulled on a hat and mittens and headed outside beyond the charred remains of the barn.

"Ethan?" She cupped her hands to her face. "Molly! Cole!"

She listened and then crossed the old pony corral and let herself out into the ten acres of timber, watching for any sign of movement.

Worry began to grip her heart in a tight vise. Ethan had been a soldier for thirteen years. How could he get lost in a ten-acre wooded pasture? How could they all be missing?

She called out to them again. This time she heard Molly's faint response and she hurried in that direction, thankful she'd thought to stuff her cell phone in a jacket pocket in case she had to call for help.

Over the next rise she gasped in relief. Molly and Cole were trudging toward her, struggling to make it through the deep snow. They both looked exhausted.

She enveloped both of them in a group hug. "I was so worried about you two. Where have you been—and where is Ethan?"

Molly's lower lip trembled. "We don't *know*. We were hunting for a tree and suddenly he was gone. We called and called and tried to find him, but then it was getting dark and we had to try to get h-home. What if something got him—like a bear?" She cast a fearful look over her shoulder. "What if it's still out there and it's coming af-after us?"

Hannah brushed a kiss against her forehead. "There definitely are bears in Wisconsin, but I haven't ever seen one on my property, and there haven't been any reported in this area for years."

She called Ethan's name several times. "You know what? I'm going to get you two up to the house and then I'll come back out and try to find him. Okay?"

Panicked, Cole gripped her arm. "No—I don't want you to. Please don't leave us there!"

"Don't worry, sweetie. It'll be fine." She gave him another hug then moved a few steps away and yelled Ethan's name again.

A shadow stumbled through the trees, too indistinct to make out for sure, but she held her breath, praying it was him. If it wasn't, how could she ever find him in the dark?

He drew closer and she blew out a breath in relief. "Thank goodness, Ethan. We were so worried! Where have you been?"

"I...don't know." His words were strangely slow and measured, as if he had to think about each one. He was limping badly.

In the dim light his face was oddly dark on one side. But it wasn't until she'd hurried to his side that she realized what it was. Blood, still dripping from a gash hidden somewhere in his hair.

"Come on, kids, we're going for a ride." She hooked her arm under his and walked him slowly into the house to grab her purse, then pulled her car keys from her pocket and loaded everyone into her car. "ER, here we come."

Ethan leaned against the headrest, his eyes closed.

He'd heard Hannah call the ER on the drive into town. He'd started to protest and then had lost his train of thought.

But now they were suddenly at the hospital and she'd pulled up under the overhang at the ER entrance. A nurse pushing a wheelchair barreled out of the automatic glass doors and she was bearing down on his side of the car.

His fuzzy thoughts began to clear as his alarm grew.

"Wait—I don't need to be here," he protested as the nurse wrenched open his door and reached for his seat belt buckle.

Hannah rounded the front of her vehicle and took his arm. "Maybe not, but do me a favor and let Ann take you inside. Let's get you cleaned up a bit—you might need a couple of sutures."

Sutures. He could handle that. He awkwardly transferred into the wheelchair, wincing at the stab of pain in his knee as he pivoted.

Hannah bent into his field of vision and took his good hand in hers. "Ethan, I need to take the kids over to Keeley's house, but I'll be right back. Ann is a great nurse and Sophie's husband, Dr. McLaren, is here, so they'll start checking you out, okay?"

She straightened, turned away from him and lowered her voice. "He was disoriented when I found him, and seemed unusually drowsy on the way here. He's a soldier on medical leave…with a history of TBI. Recently discharged from Walter Reed."

Ethan looked back at the Subaru, where Molly's pale, frightened face was pressed against the back window. His thoughts snapped into crystal-clear focus.

He started to get out of the wheelchair. "I just need to get back to my cabin. A little sleep and I'll be fine."

"Not the best idea, sir. Not with a head injury." The nurse pressed him gently back down and wheeled him through the glass doors into the blinding light of the ER, and on to an exam room where a man was already waiting.

"I'm Dr. McLaren," he said crisply. "I hear you've had an adventure tonight."

"I took my niece and nephew out into Hannah's timber to look for a Christmas tree. I slipped in the snow and fell. Nothing more than that."

"Did you ever agree on one?" The doc's mouth quirked into a brief smile. "My family never does. I finally learned it involves a lot less mileage to check out the Christmas tree lots instead of tramping through Hannah's woods with a saw."

Ethan laughed at that, which made his head start to pound. "I'm sure coming here was just a waste of your time."

"We still want to have a look. Ann is going to take your history and get that laceration cleaned up so we can take a better look. In the meantime, I need to check on another patient here in the ER, but I'll be back shortly."

The nurse returned with a laptop computer on a rolling stand, helped him up on a gurney and cleaned up his face with deft, gentle fingers. She applied a dressing and then began peppering him with questions about his medical history and medications, her fingers flying over the keys with every answer.

Next she began a lengthy assessment of his orientation, motor response and balance, an all-too familiar litany of procedures that he'd been through more times than he could count.

"Well, sir," she concluded with a warm smile, "the doctor is busy with something right now, but he should be with you shortly. Hannah's friend lives close by, so I'm sure she will be back soon."

After pointing out the call light and handing him a TV remote—not a good sign regarding how long he might have to wait—she disappeared.

Hannah appeared at the side of his gurney. "You've been asleep," she murmured. "How are you feeling? A little dizzy?"

Asleep? He glanced up at the large clock on the wall, though now he wasn't sure about the time he'd arrived. With Hannah hovering over him like a worried hen, he wasn't going to ask.

Footsteps entered the room and now Dr. McLaren

was on the other side of the gurney flipping through several pages on a clipboard. "So, tell me your name."

He rolled his eyes, though he knew it would be faster to just go along. "Ethan Williams. It's December second, and I'm here because of a minor thump on the head. And...I'm fine."

"I see that you're on no meds. No chronic diseases. Blood pressure, temp and pulse are fine. You've been through quite a bit, though." McLaren studied Ethan's prosthetic hand. "Amazing what they can do these days. How are you doing with this?"

"Well enough. Though my niece Molly might beg to differ. She asked me to re-braid her hair after I brought her and Cole to Hannah's after school. I couldn't do it without the tactile sense for managing something so fine and slippery."

"You could in time—it's just another new skill to work on." He looked down at the clipboard. "So...about your head. You said you didn't lose consciousness after your fall—at least that you were aware of. Right?"

Ethan nodded.

"Good. Your Glasgow score was 15 when you first arrived, and also ten minutes ago. Since 15 is normal and 3 is dead, you're at the best end of the spectrum there." McLaren studied him over the top rim of his glasses. "While you've been waiting here, have you had any bouts of confusion? Disorientation? Nausea?"

Ethan shook his head.

"You were a little foggy when you arrived—you didn't respond to several questions and appeared to be hypersensitive to the lights. That's not surprising with a mild concussion. But as far as tests go, an X-ray wouldn't be of benefit with minor head trauma."

"So I'm done here?"

"At this point, your assessment results don't indicate a need for a CT scan, either. But given your history of a blast-related TBI, I want to keep you overnight for observation. I also need to do a little suturing, and then we can move you into one of the hospital rooms just down the hall."

After the doctor left the room, Hannah stepped back to his side. "I'm so sorry. I feel responsible for this. If I hadn't mentioned finding a Christmas tree, this wouldn't have happened."

"If I'd been more careful, it wouldn't have happened," he retorted. "I'm just sorry the kids didn't find their tree."

"No matter. What really matters is that you're all right." She smiled down at him but her eyes were filled with concern. "I need to pick up Molly and Cole, then I want to slip into the back of the church for the last part of the Advent service if we can. Afterward I'll need to get them home for bed, but the staff here knows they can call me at any time."

She put his cell phone on his bedside table. "And here is your cell, if you need to reach me."

Staring at the stark, white walls of the exam room, he realized that as soon as she left, he was going to miss her. A lot.

"I'll be back in the morning as soon as I drop the kids off at school," she continued. "Don't give the staff any trouble, okay? If the docs decide you do need a CT or something, don't give them any grief. Both Dr. McLaren and Dr. Talbot are excellent physicians and they know what they're doing."

"Fine," he grumbled.

Her eyes sparkled with sudden humor. "I'm sure you will be. I'll hear about it if you're any trouble."

She leaned over and kissed his cheek. Hesitated, then gave him another kiss that brushed his mouth and lingered, sending a dizzying rush of warmth straight to his heart.

Then she was gone.

Chapter Fourteen

What in the world had she been thinking? Hannah tightened her grip on the steering wheel, thankful for the darkness that hid the deep blush burning its way up her cheeks from the kids sitting in the backseat.

She'd kissed him. Despite knowing full well that he was a heartbreaker. The kind of guy who didn't stay around. And it hadn't been just the light, good-luck kiss of an acquaintance, either.

She'd done it at the hospital, where any passer-by might have seen her, taken note, and then happily shared the observation at the coffee shop tomorrow morning, which would then set the rumor mill on fire.

That, she could handle with an offhand dismissal and a shrug. Eventually.

But far worse, she'd crossed an invisible boundary between Ethan and herself. One that had placed any romantic feelings between them squarely in the past.

And in doing so she'd stirred up the old emotions that she'd been denying since the day he arrived.

He wasn't just a threat to the secure, permanent home she longed to provide for the children. He was also a threat to her heart.

But he was here because of the children. Not her. And in a few weeks he would be gone. She'd best not forget that.

Hannah drove up the snowy side streets toward the Aspen Creek Community Church perched on a hill overlooking the town. High snowbanks left by the snowplows at the street intersections made each one an adventure, when she could only ease forward and hope no one else was coming.

"I never seen snow like this at home," Cole said from the backseat. "When can we go sledding?"

"Tomorrow," Hannah promised as she pulled into a parking spot at the far end of the church parking lot. "But only if we have time after choosing our Christmas tree."

"We'll be fast. I *promise*. Maybe we can go find one tonight and then go sliding right after school?"

Hannah chuckled. "It's already dark out. Too late. But we'll make sure you have plenty of time tomorrow."

She led the kids across the parking lot to the steps leading up to the church, struck as always by the simple beauty of its tall, old-fashioned white spire reaching toward the sky.

The welcoming light from within shone through the stained glass of the dozen tall, arched windows that marched down each side of the building. "Isn't it beautiful?" she asked. "I always feel as if I've just come home."

Even with the strains of "Joy to the World" floating from within, Molly lagged behind, the grim set of her mouth more suited to the gallows than a lovely old church.

Inside, Hannah collected a bulletin from an usher and led the way to a back pew. They'd arrived too late for the brief Advent sermon and most of the service, except for a soloist and one more hymn, but the dimmed lights and the candles glowing at the front of the church still filled her with a familiar sense of peace.

She glanced at Molly's stony expression and closed her eyes. *Please, Lord, help me reach this child. Her burdens are so heavy right now. I can't even imagine her sense of grief and loss, and I only want to do what's right for her and her brother. Please.*

Pastor Mark stepped out in front of the altar. "Welcome to our visitors and members. We hope you'll join us downstairs after every service for refreshments and the chance to get to know each other better. Blessings and peace to you all, now and always."

He moved back to his seat behind the pulpit and a haunting a cappella, crystalline voice rose from the choir balcony. "Mary, did you know, that your baby boy…"

A complete hush fell over the congregation. Not so much as a paper bulletin rustled.

Except for the smallest, muffled sob next to Hannah. Molly, her face crumpled with raw grief, tears streaming down her face.

Tears filled Hannah's eyes as she pulled the child into her arms and held her close, rocking her as she would a baby as Molly's tears fell and her shoulders shook with her silent sobs.

Cole edged closer, his heartbroken gaze pinned on his sister. Hannah shifted and slid an arm around his narrow shoulders, too.

"This was Momma's favorite song," he whispered sadly. "She always sang it to us at Christmas. Then she kissed us and said we were *her* babies, and she loved us more than the whole world. Only she can't do it anymore."

His words felt like a blow to Hannah's heart. "A mother loves her babies forever and ever, honey," she whispered, kissing the top of his head. "When you hear that song, think of her singing to you from heaven."

The soloist finished and the pastor led the congregation in prayer. Then the organist started a prelude to "O Holy Night" and everyone stood for the final hymn.

Molly's tears faded to hiccups and she started to pull away, but Hannah gave her an extra squeeze before letting her go. "Are you all right, sweetheart?"

Molly rubbed at her face with her hands and looked away.

"I know this has been hard—terribly hard," Hannah whispered. "But I promise you that things will get better. It just takes a lot of time."

Molly didn't answer.

"We can just go home or we could slip into the bathroom downstairs right now and let you wash your face. Then we could stay a little while," Hannah coaxed, hoping her plan wasn't a big mistake. "There'll be all sorts of Christmas cookies and treats down there, with cocoa and punch. Would you mind—for just a few minutes? It might be fun."

Somber now, Cole nodded.

Molly heaved a deep, resigned sigh.

With another verse of the hymn left, Hannah slipped out of the pew, led them downstairs and waited while Molly went into the bathroom to wash away her tears.

The congregation was pouring down the stairs when Molly came out and moved to Hannah's side. "Let's get in line, so you can pick out some cookies, okay?"

Molly shook her head. "I just want to go home."

At Cole's pleading look, Hannah tipped her head toward one of the tables. "Cole wants something. If you want to wait right there, we'll join you in a minute."

A vaguely familiar girl looked at Molly from across the room then turned to grab the arm of a younger girl standing next to her and they both came over. "I'm Faith. Remember, from the carriage ride? This is my cousin Joanie."

The younger girl's cheeks reddened.

"She's kinda shy," Faith added diffidently. "She's in sixth grade, like you, but she's been home sick from school this week so you haven't seen her yet."

"I'm better now," Joanie said with a tentative smile. "Faith says we might be in the same classes."

Another cluster of people came down the stairs and got in line for refreshments, including a tall, remarkably good-looking boy standing with his parents. Lawyers in town, Molly remembered after a moment's thought.

The boy surveyed the room with a bored expression until his gaze landed on Molly. He brightened and strolled across the floor to her side.

Faith and Joanie stared in awe, their eyes shifting between Molly and the newcomer.

"Hey, Molly," he said. "I didn't know you belong to our church."

"Hey, Trevor." Molly shuffled her feet, a faint pink blush blooming in her cheeks. "My aunt does. So I guess my brother and I will, too."

"Cool. So, are you joining the youth group?"

"I...um...I don't know." Molly gave Hannah a swift, questioning look.

"You can if you want to." Hannah smiled. "I keep reading in the church bulletin about all the things they do, so I'm sure it would be a lot of fun."

"We do good stuff, too. Like helping at the nursing home or reading to little kids."

Barely able to contain a smile, Hannah silently withdrew and headed for some friends in line for coffee.

This evening wouldn't change everything for Molly, but it was definitely a start.

Thank you, Lord, for leading me to come here tonight, even though we were late. And thank you, thank you, for bringing Molly a chance to finally make some friends.

Ethan had been watching the clock in his hospital room since four in the morning, trying to forget Hannah's sweet, unexpected kiss whenever he wasn't counting the minutes until the doc made his rounds and released him.

At least the discharge papers were on his bedside table, but he still needed Hannah to spring him from jail.

Which led him right back to thinking about Hannah's kiss.

He was sure she'd meant it as a friendly good-night and nothing more.

But trying to forget the warmth of her lips on his was like trying to ignore fireworks on the Fourth of July, because now his thoughts were spinning with a kaleidoscope of memories of those weeks they'd shared years ago.

Since his arrival in Wisconsin he'd carefully focused on the children. Tried to avoid the inadvertent meeting of accidental glances. Dodged the unintentional brush of a hand that might reawaken the fierce chemistry that had once been between them.

He snorted under his breath. It hadn't taken a touch

or a glance or a casual kiss. Just arriving that first day and seeing Hannah at her front door had brought it all rushing back, and more. She, on the other hand, had seemed unaffected—beyond her deep concern about the children.

After seven months in Ward 57 in Walter Reed, every whiff of disinfectant, every squeal of med cart wheels on the polished floors, every glimpse of a uniform set his teeth on edge and made his stomach twist.

If not for the fact that he had no car here at the hospital and no keys for his cabin, he would've left the hospital hours ago, as soon as the hall lights dimmed and the third shift came on duty.

At nine o'clock sharp his cell phone rang. Expecting Hannah, he did a double take at the Dallas phone number on the screen. David Benson, a high school acquaintance who had joined the marines the same time Ethan had chosen the army.

"Hey, buddy, I heard you had some tough luck."

Ethan leaned back against the pillows and closed his eyes, wishing he hadn't taken the call. "I'm good."

"Not what I heard from Tommy Joe. He says you were in quite a blast last spring. Lost some of your moving parts."

Ethan let his thumb hover over the off button on his phone, then reconsidered with a sigh. "I'm a bionic man, my nephew says. Just a hand."

David whistled. "Tough luck."

"That would be the guys who didn't get to come home. I'm all right."

"I s'pose it's too early to say if you want to get back to active duty."

"Some do, with prosthetics," Ethan shot back. The

defensive note in his voice made him cringe. "I'm not yet sure about what I'll do."

"True enough, but I wanted to run something past you, buddy." David cleared his throat. "I didn't re-up this last time around. I wanted to be closer to my kids. See them grow up. Another marine and I have a business here in Dallas, and we need a couple more guys with the right military background—ASAP. I thought of you first."

"Doing what?"

"Personal protection. Bodyguards. High-security courier services, and so forth."

Intrigued, Ethan leaned forward. "You've actually got this business running?"

"Six months. We can't keep up, to tell the truth. Both of us are working fifty-sixty-hour weeks and have turned away business, so it's time to expand. Interested?"

A few weeks ago Ethan would have said no. Getting back into active duty was the only thing he knew. The only thing he was good at. But now, with Molly and Cole and the custody issue, he was no longer sure.

And then there was Hannah.

Where their relationship was heading was still a guess—he doubted she would give him her trust easily after he'd so cruelly jilted her years ago, and every time he saw her, he regretted his stupidity even more. How could he have thrown away something that precious?

But he still needed to think about career options. And, if he found there was no chance at all with her, he wouldn't care what he did or where he had to live. Nothing else would matter.

"So this job would be in Dallas?" he asked cautiously.

"For now, but we're thinking about expanding into other big-city markets."

"Minneapolis–St. Paul?"

"Very likely."

"Wisconsin?"

"Uh, maybe. The bigger cities might be possible, if that's something you'd want to develop sometime in the future."

Ethan grabbed a piece of paper and a pen from the bedside table and began taking notes as David launched into an extensive description of the business, its clientele and future plans.

"So," David said after pulling in a slow breath. "Sound interesting to you?"

"I guess so."

"I'm going out of town next week, but my schedule is open on the fifteenth and I could meet with you that afternoon if you can get down here."

"I'll give it some serious thought."

At a light rap on the door Ethan ended the call and straightened, expecting Hannah.

A middle-aged woman in a dark skirt and cranberry sweater walked in instead. She approached his bedside and briskly shook his hand. "Georgie Anderson, Social Worker."

He sank back against the raised head of his bed, wishing he'd feigned sleep, but he didn't have the heart to order her out of his room. She looked like the quintessential cookie-baking grandma.

"I understand you had a bit of a fall yesterday, but

you're going home today. Wonderful news," she said. "You're feeling back to normal?"

Like he would admit to anything that might keep him here longer? "Yes. All good."

"To get right down to it, Dr. McLaren asked me to come by before you leave. He wanted me to drop off some brochures about the local veteran's support groups, as well as the VA clinic in Maplewood."

Now that he looked a little closer, she was more like a ruler-toting schoolmarm than someone's sweet old grandma. He sighed, gestured toward his bedside table. "I'll look at it later."

"Somehow, I doubt that. Dr. McLaren is concerned about you. Not just your concussion yesterday, but about what you've been through in the service. When you two talked last night, you were open about the problems you face with PTSD and said that you've rejected help in the past."

He'd said that? He blinked. The woman's voice faded into the background as he mentally reviewed the hours since he'd been brought into the ER. Sure, he'd been a little foggy—not uncommon after even a mild concussion. But when had he ever talked about his PTSD— much less to a veritable stranger?

She rested a hand on his forearm and drew him back to attention. "You aren't the only one facing this. One of our groups has a member who suffered for twenty years on his own. Refused to acknowledge that burden. Refused help. He says he never realized what was wrong in his life—he just figured he was a failure at jobs, at relationships. He never knew he could feel so much better, until he finally ditched his stubborn pride and began dealing with his problems. He's now the leader of the Saturday morning group here at the hospital, in case you're interested."

Her offer was calm and professional, but the glint in her eyes held a different message.

So was he finally ready to try?

Chapter Fifteen

Hannah checked the slow cooker, with chili simmering away in the kitchen, turned on the oven light to check on the corn bread, then returned to the living room and studied the freshly cut Christmas tree.

She'd been right.

With the lure of finally going to the sledding hill at Aspen Creek Park, Molly and Cole had converged on a nicely shaped blue spruce within fifteen minutes, had taken turns sawing at its base and had both helped drag it to the house.

The sledding hadn't lasted long given the minus-five-degree windchill. But they'd both stuck it out for five runs down the longest hill before happily heading back to the SUV to defrost with a thermos of hot cocoa on the way home.

At a knock on the door Cole ran to the front and peered out the sidelight window. "It's Uncle Ethan!"

Cole unlocked the door and opened it wide. "We went sledding! And we got a tree!"

Ethan laughed as he shucked off his boots and coat and brought a square bakery box into the kitchen and handed it to Hannah. "Dessert—since you invited me for supper. I hope someone here likes chocolate."

"No doubt about it." She eyed him closely. He'd looked pale and drawn when she'd picked him up at the hospital and had taken him back to his cabin this morning, but at least now his color was better. "How's that head of yours?"

"Fine."

"No headache?"

"I'm good."

Which was a non-answer if she'd ever heard one, but it was his business, not hers. "Glad to hear it, but I hope you've been taking things easy."

He winked at her. "Followed doctor's orders, as always."

His dimples deepened whenever he smiled, and that twinkle in his eyes made her heart take an extra beat. It was getting harder to remember that he might be polite and friendly, but he was staying in town "at least until Christmas," because he wanted to connect with Molly and Cole and then try to gain full custody. It wasn't because he was her friend…or anything more.

So why on earth had she kissed him last evening at the hospital? She still couldn't get that out of her thoughts.

It didn't take much analysis, she realized. She was drawn to him more now than she'd ever been. An indefinable magnetism hummed between them like an invisible force.

But it was more than that. With every passing day that he was here, she found more things about him that drew her. His kindness. His warm affection for the kids. The way he was so willing to help out with anything—

even to the point of taking a terrified stray to the vet clinic.

He was so different from the guy he'd been at twenty-one. His years in the military had matured him into a solid, dependable man who seemed trustworthy. Safe. Could things between them actually work out this time?

He turned back to living room and studied the tree. "Where was that one hiding yesterday? It's perfect."

Molly, sprawled on the floor in front of the fireplace, looked up from her homework. "Aunt Hannah said we had to wait to decorate until you came."

"Yeah. 'Cause you're taller and can reach the high branches." Cole went to a stack of red boxes with green lids. "Can we start now?"

"Supper first." Hannah set four salads and the corn bread on the round oak table in the kitchen. "Have a chair, then we'll say grace before I bring the chili over. Would anyone like to lead the prayer?"

After a moment of silence, she reached for Molly's hand on her left and Ethan's hand on her right. When everyone was connected, she bowed her head. "Thank you, Lord, for this wonderful day. For Ethan's good health and release from the hospital. For the friends Molly has made, and the ones whom Cole will meet soon. For this meal, and for the coming celebration of your birth. In Jesus's name we pray, amen."

Just as she finished serving the chili, someone rapped on the front door. "Excuse me, I'll be right back."

Ethan followed, hovering protectively at her shoulder, a soldier ready to take out an enemy. "I can answer the door, if you'd like."

Through the window she saw a portly man with a briefcase and a clipboard in the crook of his arm. "It's all right. I know why he's here." She hesitated then opened the door. "Can I help you?"

"Fred Larsen. I'm here to follow up on a complaint regarding your rescue facilities." His wary gaze lifted to survey Ethan. "Uh, if it's not…um, inconvenient."

"I've been expecting you." Hannah dredged up a smile. "I know you can't say, but I've no doubt it was called in by Gladys Rexworth. She has never actually set foot on this property, but she heard about the fire here and probably made assumptions. She told me that she would be calling your office."

Apparently satisfied that the chubby man was harmless, Ethan left to rejoin the kids at the kitchen table. The inspector watched him go, then seemed to recover his composure. "Can I see your animal facilities, please?"

"No problem at all. If you haven't had supper, you're welcome to join us."

"Thank you, but I'd better proceed." He referred to his clipboard. "I'll need to see your records regarding vet care, intakes and adoptions. But first—how many animals are here right now?"

"Three cats and two dogs living in the house. There was a fire in the small barn out back last Sunday, attributed to an electrical short. The inspector thought it was probably due to mice chewing on a wire."

"Any animal deaths?"

"It was basically a pony shed and hay storage, and a place to keep three chickens that were left here. They're all fine—just temporarily in the garage. We're also starting to think about fund-raising for a centralized shelter in town."

The man's eyebrows rose. "Wait—you have chickens and a pony in the garage?"

"Plus twelve puppies and their mother, who was dropped off here a few days before she whelped. Obviously, I'm not parking my vehicle in the garage anymore. Someone dropped off another dog on Monday, but she's at the vet right now, in terrible shape."

"She'll be euthanized?"

"Absolutely not. She's emaciated, and she was clearly abused, but she'll be fine with good care. If you want to check in on her, she's at Dr. Leighton's clinic in town."

"I see."

Hannah led the way into the garage. He walked from one pen to the next, noting food and water dishes and studying the dimensions of the pens. "This all is fine, but the regulations for dogs also require daily exercise and contact with people. How are you handling that?"

"The backyard is fully fenced, so I turn the adult dogs out four times a day, and the pony has a small pasture. The pups have been going out with just their mom, unless the weather is bad. Socialization is inside the house with me, and now, also with my niece and nephew." She smiled. "When we go back into the house, I'll let Lucy go outside and show you what we do with the pups. Are you done out here?"

He wrote a few more notes on his paper then nodded.

"My big-ring notebooks for shelter activities are on the kitchen counter by the phone. Feel free to look through them all. I'll be inside in just a second."

A few minutes later she peeked through the kitchen door. "Here they come—everyone ready?"

Cole and Molly had finished their supper and were back in the living room with Ethan. Giggling, they both sat on the area rug as the flood of puppies poured through the door.

Startled, the inspector took a step back, then he started to laugh. "What a family!"

"I think they're thrilled to have the kids living here now, and it should help them be better family dogs when they are available for adoption. They'll already be used to cats and kids."

"So when will you add them to your website?"

"Usually at eight weeks, but that falls during the week before Christmas and I don't want to risk them ending up as impulse buys for presents. Too many of those poor dogs end up back in shelters."

He finished paging through the notebooks then shook her hand. "I think you're doing a great job, here. The animals are all at excellent weight. The pens are clean and comfortable. Congratulations on a job well done."

After he left, Molly gently swept aside the puppies wrestling on her lap and went to the kitchen, where Hannah was eating her chili at the counter. "What did he mean about your website?"

"Well, we need to spread the word about adoptable animals, so three of us in town maintain a website showing all of the available animals. People can call or email if they are interested in one in particular, then make an appointment to see it."

"Just like that? They pick one and take it home?"

Hannah smiled at her concern. "It's definitely not just like that, I promise. They have to fill out a long form and prove they either have a fenced yard or use a buried fence and radio collars to keep dogs at home. We never want to send a dog to a place where it will spend its life chained outside. That's horrible. Dogs are pack animals and crave being with people or each other."

"Wow. Can I see that website?"

Hannah put her chili bowl in the sink. "Sure."

With a few clicks she reached the Aspen Creek Rescue site. "Here…do you want to look through it?"

Molly settled on a tall stool at the breakfast bar and wandered through the site, then clicked on Available Animals. She looked up at Hannah in horror. "Penelope is here. You *can't* send her away!"

"That's what we do, sweetie. Keep strays or discarded animals safe, and rehabilitate the ones that need a new start. Then we try to find them a forever home. It's really hard sometimes. But it's good to know when an animal will finally be with someone who loves them."

Frowning, Molly scrolled down farther. "And Lucy? Her *puppies*? You can't!"

"If you check closer, you'll see they are listed as unavailable until after January first, not now. Just think about it, Molly. Eventually that would be a total of thirteen big dogs. How could I ever keep them all? It would be a big pack eating me out of house and home. And none would have the same love and attention as if they had their very own family."

Molly shot a look at Cole, who was lying on the floor drawing pictures with Maisie sleeping at his side, then she directed a fierce, accusing glare at Hannah. "Even Maisie is in here," she demanded in outrage. "How could you do that? My brother *loves* her. Doesn't that matter? I suppose you're going to put poor Belle on the list next."

"You are absolutely right about Maisie. He not only loves her, I know he needs her. Especially right now. It's been so busy around here this past week that I wasn't even thinking about the website." Hannah pulled the computer over and deleted Maisie's listing. "There. Done. Now—let's go decorate the tree before it gets too late."

* * *

An instrumental Christmas CD provided soft background music as Ethan wound the final string of white lights around the tree, plugged it into the surge protector with the others and flipped the switch. The tree came alive with a bright glow—as if covered in stars.

Cole stared at it in awe. "It's the prettiest *ever*. And it smells so good!"

"Now we need to open those other boxes and hang the decorations," Hannah said. "But, first, here are the ones you kids picked out at the Christmas Shoppe. Maybe they should go on first so you can find the very best spots."

She handed them over and watched the children ponder their great decision. Then each hung their decoration at eye level. "Absolutely perfect."

Ethan watched as three big totes were opened and the ornaments added to the tree one by one, the kids entranced by the sparkling, shiny baubles. Many of the decorations were whimsical animal figures, Santas and angels, some were miniature nativity sets—an array of unmatched memories from Christmases over the years—so unlike Cynthia's annual white tree with silver ornaments and metallic silver bows.

After he helped hang the highest decorations on the tree, he joined the kids in stepping away to take in the full effect. "I agree with Cole. This is indeed the most beautiful tree I've ever seen. You all did a super job."

"And now I have something else to hang up," Hannah announced, pulling a large paper sack from behind a chair. "Hmm. I wonder what these could be? I'll hand them out, then we can open them all at once. Okay?"

She looked into the sack and made a production of

lifting out something wrapped in green tissue and tied with a red ribbon. "I think this is for Molly!"

She handed it over and then pulled out a similar package in red tissue and tied with a green ribbon. "This is for Cole!"

She frowned, tilted her head, and reached into the sack again. "I think there's something else in here, but I'm not sure. Yes! It's for Ethan!"

He hesitated, so she leaned over and thrust it in his hand. The brush of her slender fingertips against his hand sent a sizzle of warmth up his arm.

He looked at her in surprise, painfully aware that he hadn't brought gifts for anyone else. A little shocked by his physical reaction to her touch. "I...I didn't realize that I should have brought something. I'm sorry."

"No, don't be. This is just something everyone needs before Christmas. Okay—ready, set, open!"

He held his own package and watched the kids tear into theirs, trying to remember if he'd ever experienced a real family Christmas—with a fragrant, fresh tree or such beautiful music. Certainly not after his mother had walked out...and before that there'd been the endless tension between his parents.

"Wow!" Cole exclaimed, unfurling a big red-felt Christmas stocking covered with dogs and cats and Christmas elves, and dusted with sparkling sequins. "Now Santa can come!"

Molly's was the same, only in green with a big silver bow at the top. Her eyes sparkled when she looked up. "It's so *pretty*, Aunt Hannah. I love it! But what about you—don't you have one?"

"I've had mine since I was a little girl, and it's somewhere in the Christmas decoration boxes. I'll get it out tomorrow."

Hugging his stocking to his chest, Cole eyed the package in Ethan's hands. "Open yours, Uncle Ethan. Maybe you got dogs, too!"

The fire crackling in the fireplace and the Christmas tree lights were now the only illumination in the room, creating a cozy, festive air. It was like being in the midst of a Norman Rockwell painting, surrounded by a deep sense of family, celebration and love. Something so foreign to his life that he could barely name the emotions welling up inside.

If he lived to be a hundred, he would never forget this moment. And he would wish for it again, every single year.

He opened the package slowly, expecting that maybe Hannah had found a stocking in camo print. But when he unfurled it, his breath caught on the lump in his throat. It was black felt, with shiny silver, gold, red and green ribbons sewn in a crisscross pattern on its front surface. "Uncle Ethan" was written across the black cuff at the top in elegant silver script.

"It's beautiful, Hannah. Just…beautiful. Thanks."

How did he begin to thank her for this evening? For what she was awakening in his solitary, guarded heart?

Chapter Sixteen

The following week passed in a blur of running errands, sledding, skating and a Christmas party at the church for the kids.

Ethan was with them more often than not, which delighted the kids and—Hannah had to admit—warmed her heart, too.

Watching him out on the ice with Cole and Molly under the lights on Friday evening, she could well imagine him as a watchful, loving father someday.

"So how's it going?" Keeley strolled up to Hannah and gave her a friendly, teasing shoulder bump. "And why aren't you out on the ice, too?"

"I've never been good on skates. Weak ankles," Hannah admitted. "I'm less danger to others if I'm right here along the fence. How about you?"

"I'm beat. I spent an hour after closing restocking the store shelves and now I just want to go home."

Keeley followed Ethan and Cole's progress as they slowly made their way around the edge of the rink, Ethan holding Cole's hand. "He's sure good with the kids," she observed quietly. "How are you two getting along?"

Hannah shrugged. "Fine, I guess. The kids seem to really like him."

Keeley gave her a sideways smirk. "And how about you?"

"It's…complicated."

"How so?"

"He understandably wants to spend time with the kids, and how can I say no to that? They deserve to know their only uncle now that their dad is gone. And being difficult about it could have a negative impact when custody is reviewed."

"No…how about *you*?" Keeley repeated.

Hannah swallowed.

"If you were ready to elope with him, you must have been head over heels for him back then. Who wouldn't, with those heartthrob looks?"

"And don't forget the charisma," Hannah added with a resigned sigh. "He drew me like a magnet and I never thought twice."

"And no one else ever compared?"

Hannah gave a helpless shrug. "No one else even came close. But it isn't just that superficial appeal. Maybe I only sensed it before, but now I see it. His gentleness with the children, the rescue animals. His quiet sense of humor. Lots of things. Important things. But none of that changes anything."

"Maybe if you tried…"

"I'm doing my best to keep my feelings out of this. Soon he'll be gone. End of story."

"Maybe not." Keeley pursed her lips. "Did Beth tell you that her husband wants to talk to Ethan?"

"Whatever for?" Turning to face her, Hannah rested an elbow on the top of the ice-rink fence.

"A business opportunity of some kind. Something

about selling and installing home security systems. Alarms, I think." Keeley lifted an eyebrow. "If it interests him, maybe he'll want to stay."

Molly thudded into the solid-wood fencing next to them and flung her arms over the top rail. Her pink hat was askew, her cheeks rosy with the cold.

"I'm ready to go," she said breathlessly. "Joanie went home and my feet are cold."

Keeley grinned at her. "You're doing great on those skates. Next year maybe you'll want to start figure-skating lessons."

Molly rolled her eyes. "I'm only eleven and I think it's already too late. Have you seen those little kids twirling and going backward? Some even do jumps."

"Never too late to start, kiddo. Well, guys, I think I'm heading home." Keeley slanted a grin at Hannah. "That goes for you, too, girlfriend. If you really want something, it's never too late."

Hannah's heart stumbled whenever she slowed down enough to glance at the calendar. Each day meant precious time with Molly and Cole, and she wanted to savor every moment. So how had the week flown by so fast?

Christmas Eve was now just thirteen days away.

No matter how much she tried to make this a happy holiday season, no matter how much she planned and prayed and shopped and baked, she didn't know how the children were going to feel during this first Christmas Eve without their parents.

It might be okay, or they could feel an overwhelming sense of loss, experience a huge meltdown and be swamped with grief. All of the long talks and compassionate hugs in the world could not replace what they'd lost.

Worse, the children's caseworker was technically supposed to come at thirty days, which fell on the day after Christmas. But the woman had just called to say she would be traveling over the holidays and would come to Hannah's sometimes before Christmas Eve.

What if she came on a bad day—when the kids were distraught and inconsolable, and could only talk about going back to Texas?

The thought of losing them tore at Hannah's heart and made it impossible to sleep. On those nights, she just hit the carpet on her knees and begged for the wisdom to make the best choices for the children and the strength to face whatever was ahead.

Hannah shook off her thoughts, finished her coffee and squared her shoulders. "We'd better get going. Is everyone ready? It's time to go get Belle."

Molly shot out of her bedroom like a rocket, with Cole close at her heels. "I can't believe she can actually come home!"

"Remember, guys. She's had to fight a very serious infection where the vet had to cut away that metal choke collar. She's been very ill, and she's still weak. She might just want to be left alone. So you can't rush her. Promise?"

Her coat half on, Molly gave Hannah a stricken look. "But today is the Advent Blessing of the Animals at the town square. She *needs* that, Aunt Hannah. Trevor and Joanie are bringing their dogs, but Belle is the one who truly needs it. *Please?*"

"And I want to bring Maisie, 'cause she's old. Can I *please*? She needs it, too."

Belle was such a wild card that Hannah didn't know what to say. She was thrilled the kids had made friends at church and that their childlike faith was so firm and trusting.

But Belle had been as fearful as a feral animal when first dumped in the front yard. After twelve days of being cared for by the veterinary staff, she might now be an entirely different dog. Then again, a crowd of strangers might be the worst possible situation for her.

"I can't risk anyone being bitten. Not you two, not anyone at the ceremony. So, first, we need to talk to Dr. Leighton about what she thinks. Unless she feels Belle would be totally safe, I just don't think it's a good idea. And it isn't fair to the dog to bring her into a situation she isn't ready for. Deal?"

Molly thought for a moment. "Maybe we could park close and leave Belle in a kennel in the car. I could stay with her, while you and Cole are at the service. I'll bet God will know that we tried, so he'll bless her, too."

"What a wonderful idea." Hannah gave her a quick hug. "I'm proud of you for thinking of it."

"Is Uncle Ethan coming?"

"He said he would try, but I'm not sure. Do you remember my friend Beth who owns the bookstore? Her husband Devlin was in the army, like Ethan was, and Beth thought the two of them should meet for coffee. I imagine they'll have a lot to talk about."

At the vet clinic, Dr. Leighton confirmed what Hannah had already guessed. While all of the daily handling had calmed the dog down, her quieter behavior had been within this close environment. Out amid the bustle of crowds and the pets brought for the service, Belle's behavior might be unpredictable.

The vet tech brought Belle out on a leash. Tentative, watchful, the dog tensed when she saw Hannah and the kids and tried to turn back to the kennel room.

"My goodness—she must have gained five or six pounds already!" Hannah exclaimed.

"Not quite, but she's doing better. She's just receiving smaller feedings four times a day, dry kibble without any canned food mixed in. I'll send home some cream for her hips."

"How is her neck?"

"Still healing, so I need to see her again in a week. This dog harness doesn't hit those raw areas so it works better than a standard collar."

Molly edged closer and the dog froze, but soon her tail began waving slowly. "I think she remembers us. Can I lead her to the car?"

"Not quite yet." Dr. Leighton smiled. "Belle had no idea how to respond on a leash when we started. She's finally getting the hang of it, but if she got away she'd be very hard to catch."

Hannah loaded Belle into the wire kennel in the rear compartment of the Subaru and then she helped Cole get into the backseat with Maisie and Molly.

"Okay, kids. We're off to the town square. I think Belle will be just fine in the back while we're all gone to the service. Okay? I just can't leave Molly alone in the car and, of course, I need to be with Cole. Can't be in two places at once."

Molly nodded. "But will she be warm enough?"

"There's a doubled folded blanket in the cage to lay on, and we won't be gone long." A parking space opened up as Hannah began searching for a spot close to the service. "This is perfect. Now zip up your coats and let's hurry."

The pastor was just starting when they reached the small crowd gathered in front of the old-fashioned band shell. "Some churches take a day for the blessing of animals in October, some choose other days. We thought it would be wonderful to honor our beloved pets during Advent, before Christmas, in remembrance of the animals in the stable where baby Jesus was born, and the camels that brought the wise men. We'll have a prayer for kindness and compassion toward all animals, and a reading, and then you can line up with your pets for their individual blessing. With a forecast of heavy snow heading this way, we won't be here long."

The pastor finished his prayer and gave a quick reading, then motioned for people to come forward and get in line with their pets.

A brisk wind now funneled through the trees, sending snow swirling around their feet. Molly snuggled closer to Hannah's side and threaded her arm through the crook of Hannah's elbow. On her other side, Cole nestled closer, too, with Maisie pressed at his other side. "I'm c-cold," he whispered.

"Do you want to leave?"

"No. I gotta stay. For Maisie."

"Well, keep a close eye on her. If she starts to shiver, we'll have to leave." She urged him toward the line of owners and pets. "I'll be right here, watching you."

At the other side of the crowd Hannah spied Trevor with his parents and a black Lab. "Look, honey—it's your friend."

Molly rolled her eyes but a minute later she edged through the people standing at the back and soon the two of them were laughing over something. Hannah smiled. Molly had joined the church youth group this past week, and it promised to be a big part of her growing comfort in Aspen Creek—exactly what she'd needed after so much upheaval in her life this past year.

Hannah sensed someone approaching on the side-

walk behind her and she felt a light frisson of awareness dance across her skin. She didn't need to hear his
voice to know it was Ethan. When he draped an arm
around her shoulders, she felt a rush of warmth rocket
through her and had to resist the urge to melt into that
casual embrace.

"Hey, stranger," he said in a low voice. "Having
fun?"

"We're here for a short service," she whispered. "I
think the kids expected to see more of their friends
with their pets, but the forecast must have kept a lot of
people away."

He nodded. "I just checked the radar on my phone.
Looks like more snow."

"Yet, who knows—it could still veer off and miss us
entirely. But if you don't want to be snowbound alone
in your rental cabin, you're welcome to come out to
my place."

"I need to pass, sorry."

This was the first invitation he'd turned down and
she looked up at him in surprise. "Maybe another time
then. You're welcome to join us for supper tomorrow."

"I'll actually be gone for a while. I need to book a
flight to Dallas."

"Dallas?" Step by step, she'd been falling under his
spell all over again, just as she had years ago. There
was something about him that drew her like a magnet
and made her think about a future with him.

But was all that charm and attention just a ruse? A
way to distract her while his scheming aunt and her
lawyers were working on his behalf?

With so few days left until the caseworker was supposed to visit, why would he leave now—unless it was

to discuss plans to convince the family court judge about Ethan's custody?

She narrowed her eyes at him. "Why Dallas—and right now?"

"I just met with Devlin Stone and he gave me a lot to think about."

"Really?"

"He asked if I was interested in a job." Ethan's mouth lifted in a wry grin. "Second offer I've had this week."

Well, she hadn't expected *that*. Hannah frowned. "Both here in town?"

"Devlin's is, but he isn't in a rush for an answer. The other offer came out of the blue—an old friend with a security firm in Dallas, and he's in a real bind. He needs someone right away, so he wants me to come down to talk in person."

"Really." Was it a real job or just a good excuse for a fast departure to Texas?

"No idea what I'm going to do, but it feels good to have offers, anyway."

"Interesting timing," she murmured.

"Why do you say that?"

She thought about the growing feelings between them—on her part, anyway. All of the time they'd spent together these past weeks.

And now, just like thirteen years ago, he was planning to leave. At least this time she had some warning.

Mission accomplished, she thought bitterly. He hadn't been here for her. With his aunt's lawyers and his newly established relationships with the kids, he'd likely get exactly what he wanted.

"Aren't you concerned about being here when the caseworker comes? I thought that was one of the main reasons you were staying in town all this time," she snapped.

"No. The main reason was to finally get to know my niece and nephew. After losing their parents, they deserve better than some absentee uncle who never shows up." He cocked an eyebrow and studied Hannah for a long moment. "You don't believe I'm coming back, do you?"

"Why would I *ever* think that?" Hannah snorted. "The sad part is that the kids really do care for you, and I can't figure out what you're planning to do. Just take off and leave them feeling heartbroken? Or maybe you're going off to finagle a victory with a family court judge in Dallas."

"And that's what you think of me," he said flatly. "I thought we had more between us this time. Something really good." He rocked back on his heels. "Guess I was wrong."

"I guess we both were," she said stiffly.

"I *am* coming back, but believe what you want to, Hannah."

Emotion clogged Hannah's throat as he gave each of the kids a quick hug then headed off down the sidewalk without a backward glance.

"Hannah," Cole called out when he reached the front of the line. Feeling as if she were in a daze, Hannah numbly went to join him.

Pastor Mark smiled kindly and rested his palm on Maisie's head. "And who is this fine dog?"

"She's Maisie. She's my best friend, and she's old. Can you help her?"

Pastor Mark blinked. "I sure wish I could, but no one on earth can make her young again. We can pray that she stays healthy and strong, and has a long life, though."

Cole nodded, closing his eyes as the pastor spoke his words of prayer and blessing. Then he tugged at Mark's sleeve before he could turn to the next person in line. "We have another dog in the car. Someone was really mean to her and we're trying to make her well again. Can you pray for her, too?"

After the pastor's second prayer, Cole beamed up at Hannah. "He did it! He prayed for Maisie and Belle both!"

She gave him a quick hug. "Now we'd better scoot so we can get back home. The wind is really coming up and it's getting cold."

They hurried through the square toward the car, their shoulders hunched and chins tucked down into their collars against the biting wind.

When she spied the Subaru, Hannah stopped abruptly. A burly man was moving around the car, peering in the windows. At the back, he glanced around as if watching out for passers-by, then he bent and appeared to be studying the dog inside the cage.

"Who is that?" Molly said. Her voice filled with alarm. "Is he trying to take Belle?"

"The car is locked. Wait here for a second."

Other people were coming up behind them on the sidewalk and heading in the same direction, providing Hannah with an extra measure of confidence. Hooking her purse strap over a shoulder, she strode boldly up to her car, her finger poised over the panic button on her keychain and her cell phone in her other hand. "This is my car. What are you doing?"

He straightened and bared his teeth in a thin leer that

displayed a missing tooth in front. Something about him made a shiver crawl down her spine.

"I was just admirin' that dog. No harm in that. Is it yours?"

"I don't care to discuss it."

"Well, it looks like a fine dog, and she's looks mighty familiar. We might need to talk again real soon." He backed away from the rear bumper. Took a long, hard look at the license plate. Then he spun on his heel and walked away.

Hannah watched him disappear down the road before she motioned for the kids to come. As soon as they piled in the car, they were asking questions.

"Who was he?"

"Why was he looking in the car?"

"Was he trying to steal something?"

"Was he after Belle?"

Hannah locked all of the doors and buckled her seat belt, then looked over her shoulder. "I don't have any answers for you, but he's gone now and we're going home. Buckle your seat belts."

All the way home she went over every facet of the stranger's appearance. Exactly what he'd said and done. Could he somehow trace her address via her license number? Police could, but he looked more like a lowlife troublemaker than anyone who had a happy relationship with the cops and could call in a favor.

Then again, what couldn't you find online these days? The old days of privacy and anonymity were long gone.

Her gaze strayed to the dashboard and the mail she'd tossed there after last checking her mailbox. Leaning over, she snagged the top envelope with her fingertip and took a look at it.

If that man had any thought of finding her, he would have no trouble at all, because her address had been in plain sight for anyone to see.

On Monday morning Connie knocked lightly on Hannah's office door at the clinic and smiled. "How are things going out in the country?"

"Really well—I hope. With just ten days until Christmas, Molly and Cole are excited about winter break, of course."

"Any special plans?"

"I promised them rental skis and lessons at the local ski park, and both kids have made some friends. Now Cole joined a church youth group, so both of the kids will have a nice connection there."

"I'm so glad to hear it. Your place must be perfect for them—all those animals."

Hannah nodded. "I hope so. Molly is talking about wanting to join the 4-H club in town, so she can take the dog project with Belle and go to the obedience classes. Apparently there's a dog show at the county fair."

"And Belle is that poor, neglected stray someone dumped in your yard?"

"Yes, though there've been no huge miracles just yet. Molly works with her every day, but Belle has a long way to go." Hannah gazed at the framed photograph on her desk of Molly with Belle and Cole with Maisie. "But, honestly, I think the dog has helped Molly just as much as Molly is helping her. It's given her something to focus on, instead of her problems, and she seems happier now."

"I sure hope everything goes well for you with the custody situation. Those kids were blessed when they were able to move here."

"I pray for them every day, wanting the best for them."

"And how is it going with that handsome soldier of yours?"

"He's not mine, that's for sure." Hannah swallowed hard, reining in her less charitable thoughts. She hadn't heard from him since Saturday evening. What did he deserve—her doubt or her trust?

Her doubt, if she clung to common sense and past experience. She probably wouldn't see him again until they were on opposite sides in a Dallas courtroom. Any fantasies she'd had about happily-ever-afters with Ethan had been a complete waste of time.

"Maybe that's something to just give over to God, too," Connie said gently.

"You're right, of course. I should be trusting, not worrying. But it's so hard to just let go. I worry every day about what will happen with the custody hearing."

"I still think you two should get together." Connie winked. "That would be an easy solution."

"Right. But I'm not even sure where he's going to settle down. Beth's husband talked to him about a job here in Wisconsin, and he had an offer from a company in Dallas. Last I heard, he was flying down for an interview."

"Is shared custody a possibility? Like people arrange after divorce?"

"The last thing either of us wants is such an unsettled life for these kids. Back and forth, summers and holidays, wrenching them away from their friends. The caseworkers say the court would not approve of that, in any case."

Connie's shoulders slumped in defeat. "So there is going to be a really hard decision coming up."

Hannah nodded. "The caseworker will be coming for her thirty-day home visit any day now. We were also supposed to have one at sixty and ninety days, but now I wonder if I'll get that much time."

"Oh, honey—I'm sorry."

"Yeah. Christmas is my favorite time of the year, but this could be the worst one of my life."

A piece of paper fluttered from Connie's fingertips to the floor and she bent to pick it up. "I almost forgot. I came down to give you this. New admission in Room 202 on the hospital side. She came into the ER late last night, and this morning she's asking to see you."

"I've got three pediatric appointments this morning starting at nine. I'll go see her when I go to the long-term-care unit after that."

Connie rolled her eyes. "The nurses would probably appreciate it if you could slip over there now. This is an older lady and she's being difficult. I believe they're hoping you can calm her down."

"Is she someone we know?"

"Unfortunately, I'm afraid you know her rather well. It's Gladys Rexworth."

Chapter Seventeen

Hannah knocked lightly on the door of Room 202. "It's Hannah Dorchester. Can I come in?"

"Please do. I want to get this over with."

She sounded as imperious as ever and Hannah could only imagine what the woman was upset about now. The food. The comfort of her bed. The size of her private room. Or, most likely, her old grievances that were never going to be forgotten as long as the woman breathed.

Hannah walked in and stood at the foot of her bed. "Mrs. Rexworth."

Gladys made a sharp, dismissive motion with her hand. "I suppose you've seen my chart and know why I'm here."

There was certainly a lot of equipment in there. Two IV poles. A monitor tracing her respirations and cardiac rhythm. A discrete catheter tube trailing out from under the blankets to a bag hanging at the side of her bed.

"Actually, no. You're with a different medical group now."

"Surely you people look anyway—just to snoop."

Hannah exhaled slowly. "Strict privacy laws prevent that. Unless I'm asked to be involved in your care by the medical staff—or by you—I cannot access your chart. No one can share information about patients outside of these walls, either. So you needn't worry. Your secrets are safe."

"I doubt that very much." Gladys glowered at her. "I thought you might be planning to stop by and crow about your little victory, and I figured I'd get it over with."

Hannah drew a blank. "Victory? Do you mean the inspection of my rescue?"

Gladys drew herself up in bed. "I have no idea what you're talking about."

But Hannah knew that wasn't true.

The woman's lips compressed in a grim line and she continued. "Never let it be said that I am too proud to admit a mistake. I guess you *might* have been right about my meds."

"If you're being honest, then I will be, too. There was no 'might' about it."

"Yet I'd gotten along just *fine* for all those years."

"I wasn't sure why someone had written all of those prescriptions for you. Maybe you got them from several sources. But I could not, with good judgment and concern for your safety, renew them, and no doctor in our practice would do so, either. If I remember correctly, there were some powerful sedatives and pain meds that posed serious interaction problems. And the doses were far too high."

"My arthritis and back pain are beyond bearing. I had to have them to just get out of bed, but no one seems to understand that."

"Did your new doctor agree with you?"

Gladys sniffed. "No. I assumed you people found

out who he was when my records were transferred, and you warned him."

"So you've been doing well on safer options?"

"I couldn't end up bed-bound with pain, so I did some research online and started asking friends who travel. I discovered that when I vacationed I could get what I needed from those storefront pharmacies in Mexico, and some of it online."

Hannah rocked back on her heels, appalled. "So you've been treating yourself without medical supervision. And your doctor probably didn't know, so he couldn't have known about possible drug interactions whenever he prescribed something else."

Gladys managed a small, stiff nod. "Which, I'm afraid, is why I ended up in the ER last night. If the EMTs hadn't come so quickly, they say I would have died."

Gladys had been one of the most difficult patients Hannah had ever dealt with, but never had she wished the woman would be harmed by her own, wrong-headed opinions.

"I'm very sorry. I hope your recovery will be swift, Gladys." Hannah glanced at the clock on the wall. "If there isn't anything else—"

"Wait."

Hannah moved back to the foot of her bed. "Yes?"

The woman's jaw worked, as if her words tasted sour on her tongue. "I was foolish to risk my health. I…I should have listened to you. And I realize that because of my pride I've only caused trouble for myself—it takes an hour's drive to visit my doctor, now. So I wonder if the Aspen Creek Clinic would have me back."

"I'll ask the doctors, but I expect we would. Just

think about it for a while, and let us know. It would be easy enough to have your records transferred."

Hannah shook her head in disbelief as she headed back to the clinic. Apparently, Gladys rarely experienced opposition, because she'd angrily retaliated for years over that medication issue.

She'd bad-mouthed the Aspen Creek Clinic, the physicians and Hannah in particular. And Hannah had no doubt that she'd been the one behind the ongoing, anonymous complaints about the animal rescue.

She'd offered no admission of guilt or apology for that.

But the fact that she'd actually admitted she was wrong was so unbelievable—on par with a blizzard in July—that Hannah was still reeling when she reached her office.

Nothing would surprise her after this.

There'd been no word from Ethan since their argument Saturday evening. Finally unable to stand the uncertainty, she'd driven past his rental cabin on Wednesday, but his truck was still gone and the lights were out. Now it was already Saturday afternoon, and his silent message was perfectly clear.

He was done with Aspen Creek, done with her. And she should count herself blessed for having avoided becoming even more deeply involved with a man she couldn't trust. So why did it feel as if a part of her heart had been torn away?

Because she was a foolish, foolish woman. One who had loved him all those years ago and apparently had never stopped.

After dropping Cole and Molly off at church for a youth group Christmas party, Hannah stopped by the feed store for more pellets for Penelope and hurried home to work on the house, thankful that Trevor's parents had offered to bring the kids home afterward.

There'd been no word from the caseworker about her home visit, but with Christmas Eve next Thursday, it could be any day now. Would the woman expect a spotless kitchen? Would she grill the kids on every aspect of their lives? If one of them complained about their chores, or the school, or their friends, would that torpedo any chance that they could stay here?

Hannah had no idea and the looming visit made her feel as jittery as if she'd had way too much espresso.

And maybe none of her efforts would even matter.

But it was all too believable that Ethan was down in Dallas, meeting with his aunt's lawyers and planning his next move once the Wisconsin home visit was completed.

She slowed the vehicle to turn into her driveway. An unfamiliar, battered pickup, its tailgate rusted to fragile lace, stood parked in front of her house. The cacophony of dogs barking inside the house was deafening, even out there.

She frowned. Who could be here now—and where was the driver? No one had called about seeing one of the animals.

A feeling of unease swept through her, yet she could hardly call the sheriff's office because an unfamiliar vehicle was there. Maybe the driver was lost. Maybe this was a mom, shepherding her child through yet another school fund-raiser sale and they were looking for her out back.

Shoving her cell phone into her jacket pocket, she eased out of her car...and froze. The burly man she'd seen looking into her car in town came around the corner of the garage. He was carrying a leash.

She swallowed hard and squared her shoulders. "Can I help you?"

He gave her a derisive glance then braced his hands on the garage door and stood on tiptoe to peer into the high, narrow windows of the garage. "I'm here for my dog. Where is she?"

Hannah had no doubt that he'd tried all the doors, hoping to break in. "You are trespassing. As the rescue center website states, appointments are always necessary, and you don't have one."

"I don't need an appointment to pick up my own dog," he snarled.

Slowly pulling out her cell phone, she pressed the speed dial number for 9-1-1 and held the phone to her ear. "I've got a situation here—an angry, aggressive man, and I need a deputy. No idea who this guy is. Yes—that's right…48193 Spruce."

"Wasted call, lady. No sheriff can keep me from claiming my own dog."

"I don't know what dog you're talking about. Did you check the website? Do you have the dog's number?"

"You had the dog in your car in town last Saturday. Remember?"

"If that's true, why didn't you say something then?"

"I don't believe in making a scene."

Not where there were witnesses. "So you decided to skulk out here when nobody was home."

"I could have you arrested for theft. Hand her over."

"And I've got the photographs and vet bills—so you could be arrested for animal abuse. Actually, my vet has her own copies of everything, and said she's turning it all over to the sheriff's office this week."

He cast an edgy glance toward the road, where she could already hear the sound of an approaching car. So maybe he wasn't so eager to visit with a deputy, after all.

He pulled his truck door open, but hesitated and started straight toward her. "Don't make me have to come back, lady. You'll never know when. Maybe some night you and those kids will be sleeping, all peaceful like, and you suddenly see—"

He outweighed her by a good hundred pounds and he was a lot taller. But she hadn't studied and taught self-defense for nothing, and his forward momentum was just what she needed.

Landing a swift, full-force kick to his groin, she grabbed his wrist when he buckled and twisted it high behind his back as he fell. Then she had him nailed to the ground, groaning and gasping, with her knee on his spine and his arm wrenched in a painful position he could not escape.

She leaned close to his ear. "Just another inch and you'll need rotator cuff surgery or, maybe, you'll never use this arm again. I won't care either way, believe me. Not after you threatened my kids. So if I were you, I would never, ever, come back."

At the sound of a car door, she looked over her shoulder to welcome the deputy.

But it wasn't a patrol car parked behind her Subaru and that sure wasn't a deputy. The pale tan car sported a round county decal on the door and the woman staring at her held a big notebook, not a weapon. And she'd been close enough to hear Hannah's every word.

The woman's frightened gaze darted between Hannah and the man on the ground, then she looked toward the wail of a siren flying up the road.

* * *

Before he hauled the intruder away, the deputy questioned everyone, including the social worker. The entire process took over an hour.

After the deputy left, Hannah gave the social worker—Liz Anderson—a tour of the house and yard, and had shown her the temporary animal pens in the garage. Now the two of them were sitting in Hannah's kitchen.

Liz sat hunched over a mug of coffee she was gripping with both shaking hands. "Does this sort of thing happen…um, often, with your animal rescue?"

"First time ever," Hannah said firmly. "I'm still mystified about why that man was so aggressive and so desperate to get the dog back."

"But she was his, right?"

"He did know about the position of several scars, but he'd abused and neglected her horribly. I now think someone finally nabbed her from his property and brought her here, hoping to save her from a horrible situation. I'll do everything in my power to make sure she ends up in a loving home."

Liz slanted a troubled look at her. "You seem to lead a very exciting and hectic life."

"No, not really. I have a good career and I take in animals who need to find a good home. But now that Molly and Cole are here, they are my primary focus. I'm thrilled to have the chance to give them the home they deserve. I hope you'll see them settling in better each time you come."

Liz bit her lower lip. "I'm so glad we are in agreement about them having a loving and stable home, but I'm afraid there has been a misunderstanding. Did you not receive a letter from the family court in Dallas?"

Hannah suddenly felt faint. "A letter?"

"The attorneys representing Mr. Williams have discussed Molly and Cole on a number of occasions, and the court agreed—to drag out this process through the next ninety days is not in the children's best interest. The plan is to finalize the custody issue by December thirty-first."

"And do you foresee the result?" Hannah's voice sounded dull and faraway, even to her own ears.

"Frankly, I can't say. I do know split custody—as with a divorce—is not even on the table, nor will it be."

"I see." So Ethan had betrayed her yet again—just as she'd feared. There probably hadn't been a job interview at all. Had he flown to Texas to meet with those attorneys this past week to make sure his plan was firmly in place?

"It's not a done deal yet, of course," Liz added in a soothing tone. "But, don't worry. No matter what happens, the children will still be here with you through Christmas and, even if they go back to Texas, I'm sure you'll be able to visit."

Chapter Eighteen

Ethan wearily drove back to Aspen Creek from the airport on Christmas Eve Day, rehearsing the words he planned to say when he reached Hannah's house.

He'd been praying a lot lately and now he started praying again—wanting Hannah to be at home so they could work things out once and for all. Fearing that she would be there and would shut the door in his face. Or that she wouldn't hear him through.

Her car was in the drive. *Thank you, Lord.*

He strode up to the door, knocked and let himself in. Molly and Cole were at the base of the Christmas tree, shaking presents and stacking them back with the rest.

Cole spied him first. "You're back!" he squealed, rushing over for a hug. "We were afraid you wouldn't come! And guess what? A big box came from Texas today, and it was all of our special Christmas ornaments! Great-Aunt Cynthia sent them. So we put them all on the tree. Isn't it pretty?"

"It sure is, buddy."

Molly ran over, too, more reserved at her age, but she looked up at him with shining eyes and hugged him. "I'm so glad you're here, Uncle Ethan! Hannah will be happy—she's been really sad since you've been gone. She's out feeding the animals, if you want to see her."

Sad? He suspected she was more angry than sad, but allowed himself a small glimmer of hope.

"I've missed you guys so much." Ethan brushed a kiss against her forehead.

Molly stepped back and gave him an accusing look. "Then how come you left for so long?"

"I didn't plan to. But things got really complicated and it all took longer than I thought. Can you kids stay in here for a while? Hannah and I need to talk. Privately."

"But then you're staying, right? It's Christmas Eve, you know."

"I wouldn't miss it for the world." Ethan tousled Cole's hair then headed for the garage with long strides.

The moment he walked in and closed the door behind him, Hannah turned around with a smile. Then the light faded from her eyes. "You're back."

"I wish I'd been here."

"I'm sure you had all sorts of business to attend to in Texas," she said flatly. "A job interview, wasn't it?"

"That was why I went, yes."

"And you decided to take the job?"

"Devlin offered me a job here. And I've been offered the job in Dallas, as well." He gave a short, self-deprecating laugh. "But I haven't decided. Yet."

Hannah folded her arms over her chest. "Nice to have options, anyway."

"Funny—until I came up here, my only career goal was to get back into active duty. But that obviously isn't in the cards. Not with my injuries. Not given what I want to do with the rest of my life."

"So you've sorted out your future, then."

"Not entirely. I went to visit my aunt to see how she's doing with her broken hip, and things went south after that."

"Really." The troubled look in her eyes betrayed her, despite her nonchalant tone.

"Hannah, I can imagine what you're thinking, but I didn't go to Texas trying to wrangle the court into giving me custody. I discovered my aunt was trying to do that all by herself and I had to stop it."

She froze. "And how did that go?"

"She thought she was doing the right thing, but the legal mess she created with her lawyers had become a tangle of legal issues that took days to work through."

"And now you've gotten it worked out to your satisfaction?" Hannah said coldly. "As you can see, I'm not wealthy enough to fight you all in court."

"That won't be necessary." He pulled an envelope from his pocket and handed it to her. "A bill for a safe-deposit box rented by Rob and Dee was forwarded to my aunt. She went to that bank to cancel the box rental and clear out the contents, and found this letter. It was written by my brother a few days after Molly was born and saved all these years. He probably just forgot about it."

Hannah skimmed the letter then read it again more slowly, her hands shaking.

Dear Ethan,
If you're reading this, something must have happened to Dee and me. I want you to be our executor, and to take Molly and any other kids we might have.
I trust you, and no one else, to do the right thing and raise them right. You and I sure know

*how tough it is to have neglectful, irresponsible
parents. I pray my kids will have a far better life.
Rob*

"So you've got what you want," she said bitterly.
"Proof that your brother wanted you to take his children
if anything ever happened to Dee and him. There's no
way I can fight this."

"But I can't believe he still meant it at the time he
died. You were just twenty and in college when Molly
was born. I was in the army and had an income, so I'm
sure that's why he named me guardian back then. But
now—with the life I've led all over the globe, and you,
with a great job and your roots so firmly planted here?
He and Dee would have chosen you in a heartbeat. It's
just a shame they never thought to write it down."

She searched his face, tears glittering in her eyes.
"So what are you saying?"

He tore Rob's letter in two and then rested his hands
on her shoulders. "I've told my interfering aunt, her attorneys and the court that I am not interested in con-
testing custody. I've signed documents to that effect."

"Oh, Ethan." A tear spilled down Hannah's cheek.
"I'm sorry for the things I've said. For doubting you."

"I admit I first came up here wanting to gain full
custody. I thought I owed it to Rob to raise his kids
right," Ethan admitted. "But I was wrong. You're wonderful with them. You're everything they need to grow
up happy and strong, and no matter what happens between you and me, that bond should not be threatened."

"So what happens now?" She swallowed hard. "Are
you leaving?"

"I'd like to start over with you. I want us to forget
our ill-fated, crazy beginning back when we were too

young to know what we really wanted. I want a chance to see where we can go—the two of us—without all the drama of child custody issues to tear us apart."

She rested a hand at the side of his cheek. "I'd like that, too."

"But it's going to take time, I know," he added. "And you were right—I'm going to join a support group—finally. And I'm going to start counseling. I don't want to be living half a life anymore. I want to be worthy of you."

She slid her hand behind his neck and drew him close for a sweet, lingering kiss. "It all sounds wonderful, Ethan."

He tipped his head. "About that heart of yours, I still want to win it. I hope to be a part of your life until these kids have children of their own and we're in rocking chairs watching them grow. So, what do you think? Are we too old to go steady?"

Her tears started in earnest now and she started to laugh. "I think you won my heart years ago and never let it go, so maybe we should set our sights a little higher. But, yes—that sounds perfect to me. And what a wonderful Christmas gift!"

Epilogue

"Are you sure this is going to work?" Keeley whispered, eyeing Molly and Cole.

Dressed in a white, eyelet-lace dress, Molly held Belle's leash tight as she smoothed the big, white bow on the dog's collar.

Cole, in a pale blue Oxford shirt and tie, fidgeted next to them, holding on to Maisie. Maisie's bow was already askew and Cole's tie wasn't straight, but getting two nervous kids and two dogs ready for this moment had been an accomplishment in itself.

What a journey these past six months had been.

"I think everything is absolutely perfect." Hannah smiled at her old friend. "I just can't believe we're all here for a day I never thought would happen."

Late-afternoon sunshine filtered through the massive oaks and maples, scattering golden coins of light over the small gathering of friends already seated in rows of white chairs, listening to the soaring notes of a violin and harp.

Everyone was here who mattered to her and her heart swelled at the joy of this moment.

A few yards away Ethan finished talking to Devlin,

then he came over to join Hannah and Keeley. "No second thoughts?" he teased as he tucked Hannah's arm around his.

"Never." She reached up to curve a hand behind his head and drew him into a lingering kiss. "I couldn't be happier."

The music changed to Pachelbel's Canon in D and Molly sent Hannah a worried glance. "N-now?"

Hannah smiled and nodded, then watched the children proceed up the short, grassy aisle to the flower-bedecked lattice archway where Pastor Mark stood waiting.

At the front, Molly turned to the left and Cole to the right, their dogs obediently sitting next to them.

"They were perfect," Hannah breathed. "I'm so proud of them!"

She looked up at Ethan and their gazes met, locked.

Ethan now worked for Devlin, and the two were planning to turn the business into a partnership. Someone had made a significant donation toward building a new animal shelter in town just last week—probably Gladys, out of sheer guilt for being so difficult in the past.

But, best of all, the child custody issues were all in the past and by next month Ethan and Hannah would be the children's adoptive parents.

Ethan smiled down at her. "Just last Christmas, I never would've guessed this day could be possible. But, Hannah, you've made me the happiest guy on earth."

He drew her into a warm embrace and a kiss that told her just how much he meant it—one that sent tingles of joy clear to her toes.

And then they walked arm in arm to the pastor and their new beginning as husband and wife.

* * * * *

If you loved this story,
pick up the other ASPEN CREEK CROSSROADS
books by fan-favorite author
Roxanne Rustand

WINTER REUNION
SECOND CHANCE DAD
A SINGLE DAD'S REDEMPTION

available now from Love Inspired!

Find more great reads at www.LoveInspired.com.

Dear Reader,

Welcome to Aspen Creek! I have so enjoyed writing about the folks in this quaint, fictitious town on the western edge of Wisconsin. If you enjoyed Hannah and Ethan's story, there are three earlier books in the Aspen Creek Crossroads series: Winter Reunion, Second Chance Dad and A Single Dad's Redemption.

I love small towns and country life. We live on a rural acreage with horses, two rescue dogs and an abundance of barn kitties—all neutered, friendly and well fed. It's such fun setting books in this type of world... and I especially loved writing this story involving the reunion of a jilted bride and her handsome soldier, who have *no* intention of ever getting back together, but want only the best for two orphaned children.

This book involves Christmas and my holiday gift to you is my favorite Christmas cookie recipe—one my family has been making for over thirty years!

I love to connect with readers and to hear your comments.

You can find me at:
www.roxannerustand.com
@roxannerustand (Twitter)
www.Facebook.com/roxanne.rustand
awww.Pinterest.com/roxannerustand
Email: roxannerustandbooks@yahoo.com
Snail mail: Roxanne Rustand, PO Box 2550, Cedar Rapids, Iowa 52406.

Blessings to you all,
Roxanne Rustand

Recipe

Super Easy Roll-Out Cookies

This recipe remains easy to work with, even after rolling it out a number of times. It's great for making cookies with children because the dough is very easy to handle.

Preheat oven to 350°F.

Cream together:
1 cup shortening (don't substitute butter or margarine)
1½ cups sugar

Add to creamed mixture and mix well:
2 eggs
1 tsp. vanilla
2 tbsp. milk

Add the following dry ingredients:
4 cups flour
1½ tsp. cream of tartar
1 tsp. baking soda
½ tsp. salt

Optional: 1 tsp. cinnamon and/or 1 tsp. nutmeg

Roll out the dough and cut out with cookie cutters. Place on greased cookie sheet, at least an inch apart.

Decorate with colored sugars, sprinkles and/or red hots before baking, or frost after they are baked and cooled.

Bake for 8-10 minutes, until golden.

Yield will depend on the size of your cookie cutters.

REQUEST YOUR FREE BOOKS!

2 FREE INSPIRATIONAL NOVELS
PLUS 2
FREE
MYSTERY GIFTS

Love Inspired®

LII5

SPECIAL EXCERPT FROM

Love Inspired.

A promise to watch out for his late army buddy's little brother might have this single rancher in over his head. But he's not the only one who wants to care for the boy...

Read on for a sneak preview of the fourth book in the
LONE STAR COWBOY LEAGUE: BOYS RANCH
miniseries, **THE COWBOY'S TEXAS FAMILY**
by Margaret Daley.

As Nick settled behind the steering wheel and started his truck, he slanted a look at Darcy. "So what do you think about the boys ranch?"

"Corey is much better off here than with his dad. He's not happy right now, but then he wasn't happy at home."

"He's scared." That was why Bea had brought him to the barn first to see Nick. "He'll feel better after he meets some of the other boys his age."

"What if he doesn't?" Darcy asked.

"He's confused. He wants to be with his dad, and yet not if he's always being left alone. He doesn't know what to expect from day to day and certainly doesn't feel safe." Those same feelings used to plague Nick while he was growing up.

"I've dealt with kids like that."

"In a perfect world, Ned wouldn't drink and would love Corey unconditionally. But that isn't going to hap-

LIEXP1216

pen. Ned isn't going to change." He knew firsthand the mind-set of an alcoholic and remembered the times his dad promised to stop drinking and reform. He never did; in fact he got worse.

"How do you know that for sure?"

"I just do." He didn't share his past with anyone. It was a part of his life he wanted to wipe from his mind, but it was always there in the background. He never wanted to see a child grow up the way he had.

"Then I'll pray for the best for Corey," Darcy said.

"The best scenario would be the state taking Corey away from Ned and a good family adopting him. I wish I was in a position to do it." The second he said that last sentence he wanted to snatch it back. He had no business being anyone's father.

"Because you're single? That might not matter in certain cases."

"I'm not dad material." How could he explain that he was struggling to erase the debt that his father had accumulated? If he lost the ranch, he would lose his home and job. But, more important, what if he wasn't a good father to Corey? It was one thing to be there to help when needed, but it was very different to be totally responsible for raising a child.

Don't miss
THE COWBOY'S TEXAS FAMILY
by Margaret Daley, available January 2017 wherever
Love Inspired® books and ebooks are sold.

www.LoveInspired.com

LIEXP1216